Trapped in Timelessness
Fallen Angels

A.A Schenna

Cover Art:
Michelle Crocker

http://mlcdesigns4you.weebly.com/

Publisher's Note:

This is a work of fiction. All names, characters, places, and
events are the work of the author's imagination.

Any resemblance to real persons, places, or events is
coincidental.

Solstice Publishing - www.solsticepublishing.com

Trapped in Timelessness:

Fallen Angels

A.A. Schenna

Dedication
To my family, the best present God has given me so far, to
Maria and to readers all around the world.

Trapped in Timelessness

Lake's Curse

The Alphas

Trapped in Timelessness

By A.A Schenna

Dedication

To my family, the best present God has given me so far.

Chapter One

The dark and the moonlight weren't sufficient to help her see everything. Brittany focused on the disgusting creature and started screaming.

It was a moment where she just wanted to faint; hoping that when she woke up, everything will be fine and the same as usual.

When Brittany saw the beast running toward Bruce, she screamed again. The fearful woman stood on the dirty roof of an ancient palace and stared in horror at her partner. She remained anxious, chewing on her nails.

The beast looked horrible. Its feet were moving in an amazing speed toward Bruce. At the same time, the terrified man seemed lost. His black eyes were ready to pop out and the expression on his face exhibited the fear and curiosity at how his luck had turned in the wrong direction. Although sweat covered his body, he didn't stop yelling at them.

"Jump outside now!"

The bloody creature was running faster and faster. The moment Bruce looked at its mouth and sharp teeth, his legs trembled. He had no more time to waste. The audacious man rushed to climb away from the danger. In a few minutes, that living thing could kill him and eat his flesh.

The human-like beast had become the personalization of irregularity. It looked like the Minotaur of the Greek mythology with the head of a bull and the body of a man. Most frightening of all was the upper side of this creature.

The view of it was so scary and nasty that none of the six people had the nerve to dare staring at it for too long.

In the meantime, the huge, black bats were flying above the heads of those not being chased by the creature, and the lack of food triggered their will to attack. Their wings were so big that one of them could cover the six people. More than twenty of them flew above the terrified humans.

"Bruce!"

"I am coming; jump outside now!"

The large, ugly beast was two meters behind him. Bruce was still flirting with death. At the same time, he was moving as fast as he could.

The exhausted man had climbed only the half distance of the rock-solid fence. He tried to ignore his panic and didn't stop using both hands and feet in order to reach the roof. His muddy fingers were searching the appropriate rocks to hold them tight, but the sharp surface cut into them deeply. Blood rained across the rough ground, which made the black, hairy beast thirstier.

The shock for all of them intensified.

Bruce heard the beast howling. His fear grew until he was petrified. However, he preferred looking at Brittany who had stretched her arm to help him. His black hair fell in front of his face. Sweat ran down his red cheeks, but he didn't stop.

The rest of the team waited on Bruce. After the battle with the beast, they would have to jump outside the strange structure in which they were trapped.

They hesitated to move on and, since he acted as their leader, he would be the first to dare the next step. The fact that they were standing approximately three meters above the ground caused them to falter often.

"Hurry up!" Brittney cried.

"Don't look at me, jump!"

Bruce was still heading up there, trying to reach the roof, but the beast was not giving up. It tried to climb up there too and kept howling at its victim, although it couldn't reach him. In a while, He was lying on the dirty ground of the roof and felt grateful to God for saving his life. The beast raked the air with his sharp claws, but missed his foot by a few inches.

Immediately after reaching the top, Bruce stood next to them and fought against the bats attacking them.

Even though he had told them to jump outside, they waited for him up there and expected from him to make the start.

***

As usual, Brittany and the terrified, teenage girls did nothing other than scream. Their hands grasped their heads while they were trying to prepare themselves for the dangerous jump. The rough ground, the absolute dark, the hot air, the huge rocks, and the dust leant to their desperation.

The young boys were doing their best to keep the bats away. They didn't stop moving their arms at all.

"Jack, Dylan, keep them away with the wood. Beat them; kick them, whatever you think. Girls, jump."

"It's too high." Brittney cast him a despairing look.

"Do it now!"

For almost an hour, a real, ruthless war was taking place. The beast was howling and smashing into the rock-solid fence that held it back, while Jack and Dylan were pushing themselves even harder to prevent the bats from biting them. Their arms were aching, their hands bled, and the pressure of the heavy, black rods against their palms caused blisters to rise

In the interim, the women had no idea what to do. Then again, Bruce was trying to keep the balance. Someone had to do this.

"This can't be happening!" the girls cried out.

"When is this going to end?" Lilly looked hopeless.

"Keep doing that for a few minutes more, boys. I will jump and then I will catch the girls, then it will be your turn okay?" Bruce was doing his best to save them.

"Okay." The boys nodded.

Bruce jumped and landed on the other side of the house. His breath came in heavy pants as he swept the dust from his blue jeans. As soon as he looked up there, he jerked backward in surprise. The drained man had never thought he had the ability to jump from such a height.

A bellow from the beast yanked Bruce out of his contemplation. He yelled at the rest and felt ready to start catching the girls. He looked around but couldn't see anything. Night still blanketed the entire area with her black veil. The only thing that he was sure of, it was the fact that they were trapped in the valley of the devil. He could see no mountains, hills, or even trees. The smell of death assaulted his nose.

Lilly, Alicia, and finally Brittany jumped and, soon, rested next to Bruce. They didn't have the time to think about their action. Either they would jump or the bats would grab them.

Now it was Jack and Dylan's turn to make the last jump.

"Do it!"

They did it and knelt, scratching their red pants and looking at each other. The blond boys initially laughed but then came back to reality. Bruce's fear fuelled their own: none was used to coming across such situations.

Lilly's optimism prevented her from ripping her blond hair while Alicia kept wiping her brown eyes. Not only did they seem exhausted but cursed as well.

The bats flew over them and then swooped downward. The panicked team ran as the nasty mammals kept following them. Out of the blue, they stopped and, then, the restless company attacked with whatever they could find. They were using all their strength and their courage did not betray them.

Bruce and Jack were beating them with their fists while Dylan and Brittany kept them away by hitting them with the rods. Alicia and Lilly used rocks to make the creatures leave.

The battle seemed endless. The bats were attacking them with their wings and their beaks to kill the six people. The scene had become completely insane and, entirely outside everybody's imagination.

The girls had changed. They looked angry and kept defending as heartily as they could. Their faces had turned red while they were moving on the rough ground like professional wrestlers. The men continued the slaughter like ruthless and unconscious murderers.

"They're backing off."

"We won!

"Not for too long, they will attack again, we have to leave immediately." Bruce remained nervous.

***

The small team decided to stop running for a while. They didn't want to waste all their energy yet. They needed a short break to breathe normally. After a few seconds, they moved on slowly. Their bodies demanded that. Their legs were cramped while their hands were still bleeding.

The girls supported each other, whereas the men were striding next to them, trying to protect them.

Their mouths remained dry; they were looking forward to finding water and food. Moreover, no one was willing to talk.

They reached the corner of the cursed palace and felt relieved. They were still walking and, after a few seconds, they started running again. A terrible noise from the gate at the rear caused them to worry. It sounded like a grenade exploding. They looked at each other and said nothing else than, "Oh no".

"We have to run." Bruce looked hopeless.

"I don't believe it!" Alicia was ready to give up.

"The beast must have broken the gate. Come on!" Bruce had to take over.

"I can't run anymore." Lilly looked at Brittany.

"I can't run either." Alicia was exhausted.

"A few more breaths, Bruce, please." Dylan was still trying to breathe.

"We will not make it, Brittany. Come on, you too, girls."

"Oh no, don't say that we will not make it, baby, don't give up!"

Bruce shook his head and his eyes locked onto hers. He realized that he couldn't do this to her. He didn't care about himself anymore. But he didn't want to let his partner down.

Brittany began crying. Her tears shattered his soul. She shook her long, black hair from her beautiful face and carried on staring at him. One look was enough to give Bruce the courage he needed. That look transformed into the motivation he needed. He would try for his love.

"What is it this time?" Alicia wanted to scream.

"The bats brought company!" Jack couldn't believe it.

"I can't take it anymore! No!" Lilly started crying.

"Relax Lilly." Brittany had to calm her down.

"Get on our backs, girls." Bruce had to do something.

"Are you sure you can do this, Bruce?" Brittany didn't seem so sure about his plan.

"Yes, we can do it." The blond boys nodded and smiled at him. Jack and Dylan were sure they would make it.

"Boys, run!" Bruce yelled at them. He was scared to death.

The women held the men tight and seemed determined to give their final shot to get rid of all these nasty, bloody beasts. Their arms had locked around the men's necks while their legs wrapped around their waists. Their hair flew in the hot wind as their muscles were struggling against impossible odds. They didn't stop shaking at all.

They felt exhausted but nothing was over yet. They would fight until they won this battle. They were determined to go home.

Brittany looked behind them. Her blue eyes confirmed her fear. She was in position to see that the beast was running and catching up to them. She squeezed her arms around Bruce's neck and prayed to God to save them.

Lilly looked up at the sky and noticed that the bats were still above them. She pulled her blond hair back and pointed at the sky so that Brittany and Alicia could see them too. The nasty creatures wanted them so much. They were being chased by beasts and by the absurd fate.

Due to a lack of courage, Lilly and Alicia decided to close their eyes. They hoped that they would escape. *No matter what, at least we tried,* they both thought.

"Don't stop, boys! Don't stop!" Bruce worried about the kids.

Brittany didn't stop holding Bruce and said nothing else until she thought about the black hole that brought them there. She was guessing without being certain yet; she was just waiting for the next seconds to come in order to make this indisputable.

The beast was almost there, and was preparing to attack and tear apart their flesh. It was only a few meters behind the fighting team but the black hole, which was ready to disappear, was in front of them.

***

The men started slowing down since they couldn't run much further. They gave everything they could, but now their strength was eager to abandon their sweaty, exhausted bodies.

"We are almost there boys, almost there, Bruce, please don't stop." Brittany couldn't stop screaming.

"Please, Jack and Dylan, please don't stop." Brittany was the only one who had the courage to talk.

The men couldn't disappoint the women. For that reason, they tried to suppress their fatigue. They pushed themselves even more.

The beast reached them. It was behind them. They could hear it howling at their backs. They could sense the air it exhaled.

In the meantime, the bats were flying higher in fear of the beast. They would reap whatever the powerful beast left behind.

"We are almost there, almost there." Brittany sounded sure about it.

The beast was striving to cut Dylan and Alicia off from the rest. Its head struggled to grab them. Mouth wide, the beast snapped and its teeth touched Alicia's long, brown hair. A burst of speed on Dylan's part saved her.

Alicia realized the danger behind her and started screaming and crying. She hugged Dylan tightly. Her fingers were hooked on his chest. He yelled at the rest.

"We don't want to die!"

Alicia released tears of hopelessness. She prayed to God.

Chapter Two

The atmosphere didn't change until evening. On the edge of a strange, rock-solid cell, the six trapped people slept. After hearing a big crowd of magpies close to them, they woke up. The memory of the bats that had been chasing them had stolen their carefree mood, bringing a return of the gut wrenching fear. They held tight their dirty hands and, if it was necessary, they would run again.

Beautiful black and white birds painted the sky giving another tone to the lonely, blue color. They could see so many magpies and looked curiously around the area. In no time, the birds had managed to disturb the entire area. It was a beautiful place. It could be paradise.

The avian's song stirred up the whole scene thus giving proof of life to something that had been torn to pieces. The friends started feeling relaxed as the tension in their shoulders loosened.

The scenery changed completely as there were plenty of birds in the sky with still more coming. Soon, all this noise and the disturbance of the birds made the cheerless company wonder whether something hazardous or unexpected might happen.

They were staring at the birds that continued their everyday, cheery activities. Six pairs of curious eyes were watching over two hundred avians.

***

The warm air was flirting with their dry, red faces, while the shining stars offered their bright light. The young woman and the teenage girls were still wondering if the memory of the previous night was true or not, while the three men seemed to be better. It was the second night they had lived the same nightmare and were looking forward to returning home.

Bruce, the oldest member of the devastated team

was still searching the location. Whatever fate wanted or not, they were determined to ignore her. All of them would go back home.

He didn't stop checking the area. His muddy hands continued lifting the rocks as his fingers carried on digging the ground. While scratching a piece of wood with his filthy nails, his anger and nerves could be seen on his face and in his muscles. As much as he tried to hide himself behind the curtain of the night, his pain was visible. His feet rested on the ground and his eyes focused on the muddy ground. All this mud, the humidity, and the scent of the giant canebrakes were driving him crazy. He wanted to scream and fight against the invisible enemy, even if he knew he would die. He couldn't take it anymore; his supply of patience was completely drained.

Bruce used to be a teacher at Bridge high school. He loved teaching mathematics and talking with his students. There was not even one moment in the past where he could imagine that he would be acting like the legendary fictional hero, Indiana Jones.

Brittany held the girls while observing the most important person in this place and, generally, in her whole life: Her boyfriend, her only prop, her Bruce. As a teacher in the same school as him, she loved her work as much as he did his. Her dimmed facial expression and her straight, black hair that covered her blue eyes portrayed a hopeless, young woman.

The chemistry teacher couldn't express her true feelings. Her role was that of the mother or the elder sister for the two girls. The only thing she wanted to do was to cry, but she wouldn't do it. That would discourage the lovely girls. She pushed herself even more without exposing her true feelings.

When Brittany and Bruce faced ugly moments in the past, they talked and comforted one another in order to find the strength to fight again. The three years they had spent together had given them a special bond.

Alicia and Lilly rested their heads against Brittany's shoulders while their tears dampened her shirt. Their curly hair covered her dirty, white shirt. The dust of hell also coated her blue jeans and black shoes.

The teenage girls remained cheerless; they couldn't find any rational explanation for what was going on. They should have been at their home and not prisoners in this hellish living nightmare.

Lilly caressed her belly softly, remembering the times when she had played with her colorful dolls on her bed. Her yellow T-shirt had been molded to her body. She felt it scratching her skin. She took her hands off her belly and let them rest on her muddy, white pants. Afterward, she looked at her secret love and remembered the first time she danced with Dylan, thinking of their song. *Please forgive me.* —that was their song. She wanted so desperately to travel back in time to get these beautiful moments back.

***

Alicia was playing with her rings while thinking of the walks she used to have with her parents. She missed those peaceful times. The moment she took off her pink blouse and revealed the pink T-shirt—since she couldn't stand the hot atmosphere of the environment—the teenage girl wondered if she would do that again in future. She used to like walking and that was what she missed the most. She gazed at Jack, remembering the second time they met and the wonderful yellow roses he brought her at school. She smiled and some tears dripped down her red cheeks, becoming one with the sweat on her black skin.

***

Dylan and Jack looked at each other, shaking their heads. They were uncertain what they would have to do next. The confused teenage boys seemed completely lost and, as with the others, they didn't stop searching for a rational explanation for this crazy situation.

***

Dylan traveled back to his home in his mind, looking on the moments when he sat in front of the fireplace just as it snowed. At the same time, he reminisced about Aspen. He would never forget the days he spent there with his family. The snow had covered everything as they laughed on the sofa. He squeezed his fists as the sweat from his face fell onto his black t-shirt. He was very angry and wondered why someone wanted to cut them off from their world.

***

Jack seemed lost in the school moments, remembering the times he was fighting about his hairstyle with his parents. *Black boy with blonde hair?* He smiled as he looked back on the first time Alicia made her first comment about his hair. "Hey! You, crazy, eccentric scientist, I love your hair!" she said, and their pure love story began. His fingers made circles on his blue T-shirt and his jaw was moving back and forth.

***

They stopped feeling lost as they looked at each other. The conclusions were the same for all of them. Like it or not, their clothes were filthy and they were dirty as well. Mud, dust, and sweat had become permanent parts of their bodies. They were extremely tired and very hungry. Their main thought was their fate and the consequences it would cause in their lives from now on.

Only one thing kept them somewhat sane. They had one another.

Time was passing and the beautiful memories stayed behind in the past. The girls hid in the weird cell where only their eyes could be seen. Although they were paralyzed with fear and agony, they were looking at the boys who were not able to think or to do something to get away from there.

Bruce stopped moving. Everybody was waiting to

hear what they were going to do next. As an inspiring, strong man, and their teacher, he was supposed to know what would be the best, safe step for them to take.

Chapter Three

"Dylan...you're shaking and your eyes..." Lilly seemed surprised.

"Run!" Dylan sounded serious.

"Jack, your eyes, too..." Alicia was shaking.

"Run!" Jack was acting like a maniac.

They grabbed the shivering girls and ran as fast as they could to find the old man who had warned them of the danger. The boys couldn't control their bodies; they were caught by a great panic, yelling at the rest. The danger made them neglect to take their things with them. Bruce and Brittany were trying to figure out what was the meaning of the words they heard. The mathematics teacher was scratching his head while his lovely partner had her hands on her hips.

One glimpse full of fear shared by Dylan and Jack worked to make Lilly and Alicia agree with them. Bruce and Brittany were still curious too, but on the other hand, they heard the old man's voice.

When they came across the terrible sight, they realized it was the first time they had regretted something so quickly. They wouldn't ignore the white hair man's words in if given a second chance.

Six people, one scream, one word.

"Run!"

The downward slope they were supposed to walk in order to step in the green cover was too rough, and the huge, sharp rocks seemed extremely dangerous. Nevertheless, they managed to cross the path with amazing speed. Their feet rose high as if they collided with their butts while their dirty, colorful clothes whipped in the air, the wind threatening to rip the fabric from their bodies. Brittany's white shirt would work perfectly as a white flag for peace and reconciliation with the powerful enemy. Lilly's hair was flying in the air and, at the same time, the sweat from their faces was falling onto the yellow flowers on the ground.

Everyone ran so fast. In no time, they managed to get down to the woods, having huge trees that looked like sycamores covering their presence, shielding them from the upcoming danger. Fear had wrapped up their emotional existence, and it was even more difficult for them to breathe. They were petrified. They'd never seen anything similar to the sight they saw before them.

The anxious girls sat on the grey, harsh rocks on the wet land because it was easier for them to breathe, while the young men leaned toward the huge, low branches of the outsized trees. The place where they were standing was like a shelter with the enormous, grey trunks of the trees forming a cage that nothing could get in. They seemed safe and felt optimistic for the time. All the members of the exhausted team had their shoulders up and smiles of satisfaction brightened their faces.

"Over here…" They were all taken aback.

"Who's calling us? Where does this voice come from?" Lilly seemed curious.

"I am here, come on…" The stranger's voice made them feel safe.

"I can't see anyone." Lilly remained curious.

"None of us can see anyone, Lilly." Bruce kept looking around them.

"Where are you?" Brittany sounded nervous.

"Follow the sound of my voice." The stranger had managed to earn their trust.

They took a few steps, then one short pause, and then a sudden fall into a cavity under the roots of an enormous oak tree. The known humidity of the ground and the presence of hundreds of roots, which looked like big snakes, combined with the lack of light, made them feel lost in a dark basement.

Lilly was looking at Dylan, feeling highly the need

for a hug. Her beautiful, black eyes were ready to deliver a torrent of tears if they didn't leave this place soon. She felt lost and was afraid for her life. Her boyfriend was very important to her, and she would never feel happy again if something bad happened to him.

Dylan shared the same his girlfriend's thoughts and was determined to protect her with everything he possessed. He smiled at her and, then, she seemed confident.

Alicia worried about all this trouble and was only interested in finding the way to return to some sort of normalcy. Jack was precious and so was she to him. The eccentric young man took good care of her. He couldn't stand seeing her sad and frightened. Alicia hid in his comforting embrace. Her fingers rubbed his blue T-shirt.

Bruce hugged Brittany and stared at the unknown man in the eyes. Brittany smiled at him and got the point. They all wished they would wake up from the terrifying nightmare, but deep inside, they knew that this wasn't going to happen.

***

A big, yellow spider on Lilly's m and then on Alicia's thin fingers was enough to make the girls scream and bring them all back to reality. After their sudden reaction, Brittany shut Alicia's mouth with her dirty hand while a strange and chilling noise came close to them, offending their ears.

The older woman closed her big eyes, swallowed slowly and silently. She suspected that they were trapped and everything was now over. Her head rested on the mud while the spider strolled along her right leg. She abstained from panic and kept looking at the arachnid.

"Be quiet and don't speak."

The man with the white beard and white hair whispered and tried to keep calm. The thin fingers of his left hand covered his mouth but they could all see a smile behind the fingers.

Balanced in front of the danger was a great challenge.

A bit later, and after making sure they were safe, they started talking. Each minute that passed allowed all of them to recover from their recent shock. The whole incident didn't last for more than two minutes but it seemed endless at the time.

They felt lost, cursed, forgotten, a mixture of unpleasant feelings was having a party in their hearts. The worst fear they were struggling to get rid of was that these feelings might become part of their lives from now on without knowing when they were going to end.

"What was that, sir?" Everybody looked at Lilly.

Dylan was shaking and his voice was trembling. He was looking at his grimy hand and realized that his silver watch wasn't in the position it should be. He forgot it in the cell earlier, but he hadn't the least of intention of going up there to get it.

"Okay, my friends, that was an evil giant." The stranger sounded serious.

After a deep breath, Bruce understood and accepted his answer while the rest of them stared at the old man.

"I haven't told you my name." The man nodded at each of them. "I am Marc, your guide through this place."

They believed Marc was joking and they were looking forward to hearing him say, "That was a joke."

"What was that?" Lilly insisted to learn more things about the giants.

"That was a cursed, dark... giant." Marc tried to avoid Lilly's question.

Brittany wanted to make sure that she heard right and looked at Bruce. She was all set to start ripping out her hair but patience was still holding her temper.

Marc's words sounded simple, but he was serious about his answers. The new members of the strange community thought that he was still joking. Alicia and Lilly smiled at each other and then turned their attention back to Dylan and Jack.

"I am glad you're smiling, particularly, you girls." Marc smiled and kept looking at them.

"I feel like someone is playing drums in my heart, sir. So please, stop joking." Lilly rolled her eyes and swept her face.

"And I feel like I had a fight with Muhammad Ali so please, no jokes, Mr. Marc." Alicia sounded like a child. She missed her family.

"I don't know Muhammad Ali, but I'm sure that we've just seen a cursed, embodied spirit." Marc wanted to let them know.

The two youngest of the new couples in the ill-fated community laughed, but Bruce and Brittany didn't. They tried to accept as true what they heard from the aged man, especially, after their meeting with death, and felt grateful to God for the outcome of their acquaintance with their enemy.

The young team was pretty lucky this man had found them in the right place at the right moment. *If only these kids knew that luck is by our side,* their teachers thought, but they preferred not to say anything.

Brittany caressed Bruce's hair while the muscular man's hands rested on her arms. Despite their age, their bodies looked so muscular that everyone believed they were both professional athletes. The first day they stepped in the school almost three years ago, all the students were pointing at the impressive couple. Lilly and Alicia believed they were in their early thirties and so did Jack and Dylan.

"When did you come here?" Marc waited for an answer.

"Yesterday…" Bruce seemed helpless.

"It's only you?" Marc gazed at Bruce.

"Yes." Marc smiled and shook his head.

The irritated company was thirsty to hear something that could make things like they used to be. That was the reason they all answered simultaneously. They seemed impatient to hear that things would change. As more time was passed by, hope was lost, and they felt helpless.

Brittany changed position and rested against Bruce's chest, Dylan scratched his nose, Lilly bit her lips, Jack ran his fingers through his hair, and Alicia twisted her fingers in a never-ending circle. They were so tense, unable to handle problems without feeling hurt.

"You don't belong here. Soon you will go home." Marc was absolutely sure about that.

"Sir, we are hungry, thirsty, and haven't slept in ages. We feel cursed. How are we supposed to go back home?" Bruce couldn't stop making questions.

"You have to be very patient and cautious." Marc sounded like their father.

"What did you say?" Lilly had no more patience.

"You heard me." Marc looked angry at Lilly. The young girl was rude.

Bruce seemed astounded; his face reddened while the rest of his team wore the color of fear looking like ripe, yellow lemons. The girls revealed their pain by releasing tears as Brittany tried to pay attention to Marc's words. Regardless of the emotionally negative atmosphere, Bruce posed more questions to Marc.

"What happened? Where are we?" Bruce was interested to know more about that place.

"It doesn't matter." Marc wanted to avoid his question.

"What?" Bruce waited for an answer.

"There is no need to know more." Marc ignored his question.

Bruce smiled as he tried to knock away one of the hundreds of roots that had scratched his back with a hand. In no time, he got rid of the nasty thing and returned his attention to the conversation.

Marc tried hard to make it sound like a funny story and continued smiling in an effort to see them determined to move on, but he wouldn't lie.

Then again, Bruce had learned to face life and so had Brittany. They both preferred living their life while facing reality than running toward utopia. She stared at her man, feeling lucky and proud having him next to her side all these years.

"Is there any way to go back home now?" Brittany wanted to know.

"Maybe..." Marc wasn't ready to answer her question.

Lilly and Alicia became upset. This wasn't the exact answer they wished to hear. They hadn't realized the real presence of the nice, old man.

Brittany held their hands and tried to make them feel strong. She smiled at them and finger-combed their hair back. Their teacher felt completely helpless. She wasn't sure what she should say next. She couldn't think of anything to do in order to help the girls.

Dylan and Jack had nothing to say either, they didn't even move.

Bruce and Brittany seemed experienced with difficult situations, but they had no idea what they were going to meet. They had been condemned to this brutal banishment due to their fate, but they had never understood the reason why they had to go through this for the past two days. Even so, they had learned to fight everyday, having an excellent contact with reality. Regardless of the changes brought to their life, they had already accepted the fact that nothing would be the same again. They had one another, and this was the best gift life had given them so far.

Jack understood now and started discovering the truth...

"What kind of place is that?" Jack was hooked on

27

his lips.

"It's a place where you are not supposed to be." Marc tried to make it sound like a fairy tale.

"What are these giants, and what are they doing in the woods?" Jack was looking forward to hearing his answer.

"Your eyes see it like that. The true color is black. The total darkness is dominating here." Marc seemed fine with that.

"What?" The four teenagers panicked.

Shock and awe formed in their eyes as their lips couldn't stop shaking. They had never thought that in a few hours, they could have experienced, seen, and heard so many unbelievable things. They were stunned and kept listening to the speaker.

Bruce and Brittany were totally cool with that. They realized that this man was different from them.

"What did you say?" Alicia couldn't understand the stranger.

"Your eyes see it like that. The true color is black. The total darkness is dominating here." Marc loved talking with the teenagers.

"Oh no! You must be joking." Lilly couldn't believe his words.

"No, I am not." Marc's eyes pierced on hers.

"How can you be so mild with that? I see you so calm..." Lilly didn't stop making questions.

"I am used to that, Lilly." Marc smiled while Lilly had to think of his words.

"Excuse me, but did you say black? I see the green, the grey colors, the flowers, and the ground..." Alicia was sure Marc was wrong.

"Yes, Alicia..." Marc kept answering their questions.

"How many giants are out there?" Bruce wanted to know.

"There are plenty of them, not only the one you saw earlier. Don't close your eyes and don't scratch your head like that, just breathe normally and you'll get over it." Marc tried to encourage Bruce.

"Oh my God…" The leader sounded hopeless.

"You don't have to be afraid, Bruce." Marc stretched out his arm and held his hand.

"Alicia and Lilly, both of you relax, please. Don't be afraid, we'll make it." Brittany had to support the girls.

"We'll all die, Brittany; we're the food for these monsters. It's pretty obvious they're extremely hungry." Alicia rolled her eyes while Brittany shook her head.

"Keep your voice down, Alicia. They can hear us." Marc decided to take over.

"So, we'll have to whisper all the time like you…I can hardly hear you." Alicia was out of control.

"We usually whisper but, sometimes, we talk loud." Marc seemed to understand.

"That's great, Mr Marc! We'll talk loud the moments these monsters are chasing us."

Alicia did a great job. Six people were laughing while she was the only one to have her mouth sealed with the chains of sorrow. After her last words, everyone laughed but soon, they came back to their revealing conversation. They had no time to waste. It was time to learn more. Alicia rested her head on Jack's legs. Lilly was lost in Dylan's arms.

"Mr. Marc, these monsters are very hungry, aren't they?" Lilly pulled her hair away from her face and waited for his answer.

"Yes, Lilly, they are."

"Then, it's over. They're going to eat us." Lilly looked at Dylan and remained silent.

"They can't eat you." Marc gazed at the boys.

"What are they doing here?" Dylan was scared to death but he wanted to know.

"They are waiting for their punishment." Marc was short and simple.

"When will they be punished?" Dylan waited for his answer.

The kids couldn't understand how Bruce and Brittany were so calm. The obsessive, teenage company hadn't realized yet that all these years, life was a battle between agony and vanity. They wished they wouldn't have to experience such painful situations. But they were going to be part of their lives from now on. They couldn't do anything to change it.

Bruce smiled and, then, Brittany leaned against his shoulder. They wouldn't give up doing their best to survive.

"What do we have to do?" Bruce whispered so that the kids wouldn't hear their talking.

"Be patient and pray." Marc whispered too.

"Is it so bad?" Bruce's eyes locked on his.

"Yes." Marc nodded at the leader.

"Why?" Bruce couldn't understand what was happening.

"You will find out that when the time will come." Marc abstained from telling him everything.

"Okay." Bruce accepted his answer.

"Are we going to make it?" Brittany was still curious about their future.

Marc shook his head and rolled his eyes.

"Are you hungry?"

"Yes." They responded all together and looked at him.

"You can eat these." Marc opened his bag.

"What are these?" Alicia was hungry and impatient as well.

"Pies and honey..." Marc put the food in front of him.

"Oh...these pies are delicious." Alicia seemed to

enjoy the food.

"The honey tastes wonderful." Jack was thrilled.

"Yeah…"

"You're lucky to have this food so don't lose your time." Marc was happy to see them enjoying the meal

The food was the best they could have. The shelter they had found was dirty and mud covered everything with mud but for now, they were safe. The experiences they had in one day were numerous. Their minds refused to estimate and make plans, as they should have done. They wished they had the chance to return home to their beds, talking and sharing beautiful moments with the people they loved. For the time being, this was unfeasible.

Only one thing kept them sane, and they retreated there, to the safety they had known such a short time ago.

Chapter Four

Every student celebrated the end of the tiring semester. Summer holidays were already on the threshold. It seemed like the best period for each young person who was looking forward to exploring the summer days and nights that could offer them the vivid experiences they needed. The sun hugged their souls and its rays covered their spirit with optimism and joy. It did its best to trigger their impatience for the unknown future.

The beautiful birds couldn't stop twittering, thus making the whole atmosphere more celebrating. It was remarkable that they were making circles around their nests built under the yellow tiles of the imposing, white building.

The smell of the apple pies reached their nose and a long lasting breath was enough to make them feel satisfied for the best day of the year. Every single person was smiling while most of them were playing games with the water. A little bit further out, some girls were drying their hair, and the impatient young men were occupied with their favorite hobby, teasing girls of course. Smiles were everywhere.

The gentle breeze was shaking the beautiful pine trees. It was like they were dancing, like engaging the celebration of the high school.

The large, green room that served as an atrium in the wonderful school had an amazing view of the forest. Lilly was amazed by the smell of the trees. The noise of the students and the sweat on her skin made her angry, but she wouldn't let this destroy her mood. The unbuttoned, pink shirt helped her look like a young goddess. She loved her school and her friends, but summer was there. Since it was her favorite season, she would go back home for a few months. However, she would miss all these experiences for a while. Lilly pulled her hair away her face and reveled in the lake of pleasure.

Some young couples were strolling in the schoolyard, talking and making plans for the summer. A small group of girls couldn't stop laughing, a few meters further away, a couple of boys were discussing the funniest moments of the year, and the same was happening with another group of students closer to them. This happy mood lasted for several hours. It was wonderful seeing such beautiful pictures of young people having fun.

"What are we doing here?" Lilly sounded like a little girl.

"Can't you remember?" Jack asked.

"Yes, I can, Jack. I remember everything." Lilly smiled.

"It was really great." Jack held her hand and she laughed.

"Yes, indeed."

"I am gonna miss school."

"Yes…"Jack shook his head.

"No…!" Lilly laughed and so did Jack.

***

After the end of the celebration, the students had gathered in the large, colorful yard. The school busses were ready for their last road trip. The countless teenagers were resting under the shadows of the large trees and talking loud.

Every young student from the prestigious school had already packed his or her belongings and was ready to go back to their families. A few last words, some friendly hugs, and then everybody sat on their seat to start the trip to their final destination. The first bus in the row had the longest trip; the only vehicle those who were inside would have to travel for several hours.

Jack, Dylan, Alicia, and Lilly were the only passengers of the first school bus along with Ms. Brittany Shein and Mr. Bruce Jacks. The two teachers would keep company with the driver and accompany the four teens home. They would have to travel almost twelve hours. With no further delay, they began their journey.

Peaceful and happy thoughts took place in their minds as they were planning their upcoming events of their holidays. A few hours later, having covered only a small part of their trip, the overweight, middle-aged driver suggested that they should have a ten-minute rest. No one seemed to have any objection.

Very soon, a small, white canteen could be seen on the edge of the forest. The students were ready for their break. They had already put their notes and plans in their bags, smiling and laughing at each other.

"Stay close and don't go far away because we're leaving in ten minutes." Brittany sounded strict and serious.

"Don't worry Ms. Shein, we will go to the canteen and be back again." Lilly reassured their teacher they would stay close.

***

Ms. Shein held Mr. Jack's hand and followed him. He was taking her under the shadow of an enormous pine tree, while she was using her right hand to put her green hat on her head. Both Bruce and Brittany seemed strict but couldn't hide their sympathy for these teenagers. The way they were looking at them showed that both of them really loved these kids. They remembered the time they were students in high school and found it very difficult not to understand them.

"That's great because I don't want to lose eye contact with you. I am pretty sure you didn't forget my all time classic phrase." Brittany was staring at the teenagers.

"I see you!" The four kids smiled at their teacher.

"Exactly..." Brittany waved at them and looked at Bruce.

It was too hot, and they were badly in need of some cold beverages. They started walking toward the canteen. The dust on the ground made them feel like they were in their natural environment. There were many hours in the school bus and the trip was tiring, but it was not over yet.

They came closer to the canteen. A sweet, aged woman was there to offer them her good offers. The whole structure was ready to fall apart, but she seemed indifferent. She liked her job whereas she neglected her safety. She had long, white hair. Her eyes locked onto the students' faces. Her feet were moving slowly. Even though she behaved with kindness, they started feeling pretty weird as she watched them all the time. Sweat covered her skin, but even so the two ladies tried to be friendly, and they didn't seem to be bothered by her behavior and appearance.

"Could you give us four Cokes, please?" Alicia was very thirsty.

"Yes..." The aged woman could hardly move.

"Why are you pulling your hair, Alicia?" Jack stood behind Alicia and started teasing her.

"It's too hot Jack; can't you see the sweat in my forehead?" Alicia swept her forehead and Jack tried to be kind.

"I can help you if you want."

"No, thanks!"

The woman brought their beverages without breaking eye contact. This was the first time they had noticed her shaking hands, but they had tried not to show it. Dylan and Jack smiled at the older woman as Lilly and Alicia tried to show their sympathy for her. The boys hid their eyes under their red hats and started laughing.

"Here you are." The aged woman smiled at them.

"Thank you." Alicia smiled too and looked at her.

"What happened to your arm, madam?" Lilly seemed to care about her.

"Yeah really..." Alicia went closer and looked at the woman's arm.

"I had an ugly cut many years ago but now I am fine. Thanks for asking and for your interest, my sweet girls." The aged woman liked talking with the girls.

We are happy to know that you're fine now. So ... have a nice day, madam." Alicia and Lilly tried to be polite.

"You, too..."

The woman was staring at them making the teens wonder whether something was wrong. The sun's rays touched her face. The girls seemed to worry about her, and so did Jack and Dylan. They were still close enough to the girls, waiting to hear something.

"Are you okay, madam?" Lilly worried about the aged woman.

"I am fine girls but..." The old woman wanted to share her secret with the kids.

"What is this smell?" Jack couldn't stand the smell.

"It's garlic."

"You should be careful because it smells awful." Jack stepped back and kept laughing.

"Jack!" Alicia and Lilly looked angry.

"That's all right, girls, maybe Jack is right. I just wanted to tell you to be careful tonight." The old woman sounded serious.

That was enough to trigger their curiosity. All they wanted to know was what she was talking about, especially Dylan and Jack. They were ready to turn back to the school bus but after cryptic statement, they stopped moving. They were awaiting her words that had already come up to her mind. They held the cold beverages in their hands, and their face expressions were frozen in expressions of doubt with a touch of fear.

"Why are you saying that?" Dylan was interested to know.

"Because tonight there is a full moon. I am pretty sure that these black clouds will appear again." the aged woman went closer.

"What?" Jack was taken aback.

"For two days, the forest has swallowed everyone

who walks down to its paths under the moon light." The old woman's words sounded weird.

Jack and Dylan were laughing while Lilly and Alicia were trying to pay attention to the old woman. The lovely girls kicked them on their ankles and stared at the old woman again. She was serious and didn't seem naïve. She didn't seem to joke. After a few seconds, Dylan looked pensive; he couldn't stop scratching his nose. Jack decided to walk back toward the bus, giving her his best smile. He looked at Alicia, and she acted the same while Lilly was next to Dylan ready to talk.

"Yeah right…" Dylan didn't believe her words.

"You can laugh as much as you want but I am not kidding, young man." The old woman pointed at him.

"Whatever you say, miss." Jack nodded at the old woman and then he shook his head.

"Come on guys, let's go back." Lilly looked back and, after a while, she started walking toward the school bus.

The four kids left the canteen looking only straight ahead, admiring the green beauty and the numerous birds.

"What is that? What happened to them?" Alicia hadn't seen something like that before.

"I have no idea!" Only Lilly was able to answer. The rest carried on looking upon the birds.

They noticed that their teachers and the driver were watching the sky.

Dylan turned back and observed the woman who was obviously disappointed by their reaction. She sat on her broken brown chair, and the wind began a battle with her hair. The woman sealed her lips and shook her head until two black eagles flying above them managed to steal her sight.

"Did you see her eyes?" Jack was still curious about the aged woman.

"That woman made me chill, look my hand! I got

really scared!" Lilly wanted to forget her.

"Ten minutes passed, come on dream team, let's go." Their teacher sounded impatient.

"We're coming, Ms. Shein." Alicia wanted to leave that place immediately.

The scenery seemed peculiar. In a beautiful location with plenty of wonderful trees, there was a yellow school bus and, a few meters farther, a small, white canteen and seven people feeling happy and stress free. However, there was also a strange figure gazing at them without saying much. In addition to that, she managed to spread fear, doubt, and terror without having an obvious reason for doing such a thing.

"Bye!" Alicia looked happy

"She is crazy!" Lilly smiled and took a deep breath.

"Completely…!" Alicia wanted to get away from there.

"Oh, yes…" Lilly kept smiling.

A few seconds later, the girls were laughing at those they had just heard without noticing the woman who was now standing outside the window. She was smoking a cigarette and staring at their faces.

The joyful team didn't believe the story that the woman had.

"Don't go into the forest tonight." The strange woman managed to surprise them.

"What?"

Lilly arched her eyebrows and stared at the woman. She shook her hair off her peaceful face, behaving as politely as she could.

"Stay away from the forest tonight." The old woman was not kidding.

"Why?" Alicia panicked.

"If you don't pay attention, you'll regret it." The old woman gazed at the forest.

"Please, stop it because you are making us

nervous." Lilly yelled at the old woman.

"I am afraid you need some serious help, madam."

Alicia tried to stop their conversation without caring whether she was polite. Her thin fingers were shaking, and she was ready to call the teachers.

The old lady's expression caused her to fear for their safety. All she wanted was to stay away from them. She got up from her seat and hid in Jack's hug.

"Stay away from the forest." The old woman didn't stop talking.

"Whatever you say, madam." Dylan whispered.

Dylan and Jack gave the answer the woman was looking for. Their conversation had finally reached an end.

The driver started the engine, leaving behind them the place and its strange, old lady. Their meeting with that woman destroyed their cheerful mood. That didn't last for long, as Jack finally found a way to make them forget their creepy experience.

***

"That woman was completely crazy; I bet she doesn't have a husband. Lack of sex can cause many serious problems." Alicia was shaking.

"I agree!" Lilly looked at her friends and smiled.

"So do I." Dylan continued gazing at the old woman.

"Me, too!"

Jack laughed and so did the girls. Dylan was lost in his thoughts, but he couldn't help laughing and started talking about work with the rest of the team.

Out of the blue, the aged woman vanished, as did the small canteen. None of them saw that as their trip carried on.

***

The trip home seemed endless. The whole scene of driving into the beautiful forest could be monotonous and tiring. Night took over and moon light replaced the sun.

39

The stars slipped on the sleepy sky and seven people traveled along with their dreams.

Lilly was holding Dylan's hand while Alicia was resting her head on Jack's chest. The two teachers were reading their books and avoided expressing their feelings in front of their students.

Openly, everyone agreed with the fact that they needed another break. A small, wooden pavilion offered them the short rest they required, as their break would last longer than the previous one.

There were only a few, tired people but there was no space for all of them. The large television had taken up everybody's attention. No one noticed the arrival of the new visitors. There was only a small, black table and two black chairs in the corner with the huge refrigerators. Everything seemed so peaceful and quiet that only the forks and the spoons clattering against tin plates broke the wall of silence.

"We'll sit somewhere outside, Ms. Shein and Mr. Jacks. You could sit here with the driver." Lilly was the only one who had the courage to talk.

"Stay close." The teacher sounded serious.

"Mr. Jacks, can't you see us?" Lilly was tired, they were all tired.

"What do you mean, Lilly?" The teacher smiled.

"We are exhausted. Where can we go? Lilly fixed her hair and bit her lips.

"Okay..." The teacher nodded at them and stared outside.

The teenage team sat on the brown benches while jokes and funny stories that took place during the school year made them laugh, until Jack saw a little squirrel and tried to catch it to show to Alicia. He went away from his group. After a while, the rest of them followed him. The night was wonderful. They found it very appealing to stroll in the woods. They started getting deeper into the forest and its seductive environment made them desire more time in this place.

"Where are you going, Jack?" Lilly waved at Jack.

"I want to see where the squirrel is hiding." Jack looked curious.

"We'd better stay close with the others." Lilly yelled at him.

"We aren't going anywhere, Lilly." Jack decided to ignore her words.

"Yes but I feel… actually I can't explain it." Lilly hesitated.

"Come on!" Jack had his way to make the rest follow him.

"Don't go too fast, Jack." Alicia was behind him.

"Yeah, boys, steady steps. Hold our hands because there is no light, okay?" Lilly was shaking but she followed them too.

"Yeah, Lilly, relax! I 'm here and so is Jack." Alicia sounded confident.

"Alicia, where are you?" Jack wanted to make sure she was fine.

"Hold on a minute, Jack! Take it easy! I can't see anything!" Alicia was behind him.

"Relax and feel free to explore the paths of curiosity, to discover the secrets of the forest…" Jack seemed to enjoy their adventure.

Alicia went with them, and they strolled into the forest looking for a squirrel until the weak light of the small pavilion was no longer visible. They held each other, laughing with the stories of their school years, ignoring the fact that they were going deeper and deeper into the woods, searching for a squirrel that couldn't be found. Time passed by, but the adventure they had decided to live, had no time, no age, no limit, nothing.

A branch cracking and footsteps coming toward them in the dark startled the teens.

"What did I tell you?" Bruce was angry.

"Mr. Jacks you scared us!" Jack was surprised.

"Why did you leave kids?" Brittany was angry too.

"It was Jack's fault, Ms. Shein." Lilly had to be honest.

"Let's go back!" The teachers sounded angry.

The moment they stopped talking, Alicia disappeared. After a while, the six people were no longer in the woods. They had all disappeared.

Chapter Five

Big, red scorpions started walking among the ashes. Every time that passed by, there were more and more coming up, trying to circle the surprised people. In just a few seconds, they could see thousands of scorpions.

A couple of minutes earlier. It was dark and now they couldn't explain the sudden change. The day light was falling on their faces while they were still wondering about what was happening. The raindrops had kept the scorpions under the jagged, wet ground, but the sun gave them the opportunity to search their territory.

Lilly and Alicia panicked and couldn't help becoming upset. They opened their mouth and started screaming. Brittany began calling for help. She was hooked on the man who was always there for her to support her and above all, to love her.

"Bruce!"

Her man hugged her immediately since it was the first time she was acting like that in front of their students. Brittany used to be calm and ready to face anything. This didn't seem normal, and she was surprised. In no time, Bruce realized her lack of courage.

The children stayed unwavering as they thought that this was just a nightmare and they would soon wake up.

Bruce was shocked and so were the rest. The picture of them was disappointing. Dust was already marked on their clothes. The unpleasant surprise of the nasty, irrational mystery was painted on their frightened faces. Their hands were shivering and sweat began soaking their clothes.

"Oh no, what did it happen?" Alicia panicked.

"What are all these creatures?" Lilly couldn't believe it.

"These are red scorpion girls." Bruce had to say something.

"Why is this happening? I didn't do anything bad..." Alicia cried.

"Neither did I..." Lilly seemed desperate.

"Girls, calm down okay" Brittany was still breathing very fast.

"What are we gonna do, Bruce" Jack remained curious.

Brittany and the girls surrendered to fate while Bruce and the boys seemed to have understood their adventure had just started. They circled the girls and didn't lose time.

"What are we gonna do, Bruce?" Brittany kept wondering too.

"I don't know, Brittany, but please stay calm and keep your voices down." Bruce was trying to think of a plan.

"Jack, Dylan, do you have any idea?" Lilly wanted to kill them.

"Not yet, Lilly, and please stop looking at me like this." Dylan felt guilty.

"What do you mean, Dylan?" Lilly couldn't control her feelings.

"Don't look at us like we are responsible for that!" Dylan was trying to defend himself.

"I didn't say that. I don't believe that you are responsible for the whole situation." Lilly noticed his facial expression and stopped provoking him.

"Then drop it" Dylan was out of control.

"Do something or say something." Alicia got into the conversation and tried to calm him.

"What are we supposed to say, Alicia?" Jack was angry too.

"Everybody please calm down."

They were all tense. Bruce stopped their conversation, they would start quarreling, neglecting that they had to face an enemy.

Bruce and Brittany had gone through many difficulties and knew very well that the worst thing they could do was to blame each other, when they were facing a difficult situation.

The children were looking at them and soon adopted their attitude. They were not enemies; they all had to cooperate to overcome this.

The real enemy was coming closer and closer. As far as they could assume, there wouldn't be any negotiations. The terrifying creatures were moving fast toward their side, and that made them more threatening. Panic ate away at their confidence and soon was part of their very beings.

"Oh no, I don't want to die!" Lilly couldn't stop screaming.

"We will die!" Alicia seemed hopeless.

***

The scorpions were too close. The small team could clearly discern them in the ashes. In less than a minute, they creatures would reach their shoes.

The girls were so anxious that they couldn't stand not screaming. The men had no idea what to do. They waved their hands at the scorpions, warning them to stay away, but they realized this gesture was in vain.

"These insects are disgusting!" Alicia kept looking at the scorpions.

"And also deadly, Alicia, they could kill us just with a bite..." Jack was doing his best to make things worse.

"I already know that, Jack, but thanks for the information." Alicia looked at Jack and seemed ready to attack him.

"Take it easy kids and don't panic." Bruce had to make them stop.

"I am sick of the dust, the awful smell of this environment and of these awful creatures. It's over, they will kill us…" That was it. Lilly gave up hoping.

"Lilly, please, calm down." Brittany held Lilly's hand and tried to comfort her.

"How can I do that, Brittany?" Lilly didn't stop crying.

Brittany got on Bruce's back, and the girls did the same thing with the boys. Bruce was fine with that while Dylan and Jack were sure they could handle it. They were the men, and they had to protect the girls.

After the way Lilly and Alicia had reacted, they managed to pass to the boys the motivation they were looking for in order to feel strong and to gain back the courage they had lost.

The helpless company was facing a flood of death. Everything was against them. They had nothing to defend themselves with except their voices. They screamed because it was the only weapon they had to protect themselves.

Miraculously, the scorpions stopped moving and giving the group a sense of relief for a while. The scorpions fled into the ground and then the atmosphere became celebratory. They all started laughing. They hugged each other but the girls were still ready to get on the men's backs, if it was necessary.

"We made it!" Alicia was thrilled.

"Did you see that?" Lilly got over the shock.

"Yea, girls, it was too easy!" Dylan looked happy.

"Dylan, I am sorry for yelling at you earlier." Alicia hugged her friend.

"I am sorry too, Jack." Lilly did the same thing as well.

"That's okay, girls." Dylan felt so lucky. He loved his friends.

"By the way, you need a shower, Dylan." Lilly started teasing him.

"So do you, Jack." Alicia pointed at Jack and

smiled at him.

"So do all of us, we smell like animals!" Brittany joined their conversation.

The women started laughing and so did Jack and Dylan. Bruce was the only one who was not hugging enthusiasm. His gaze was locked on something behind them. His expression became one of panic. His eyes and his mouth opened wide.

"Are you ready, boys?" Bruce was scared to death.

"Ready for what, Bruce, I don't understand?" Jack was taken aback.

"Run as fast as you can." Bruce was not joking.

"Why?" Dylan had no idea what he was talking about.

"Follow me and don't look back, okay?" Bruce was shaking.

The girls looked back. Their smiles vanished. Danger had managed to steal their joy. They screamed.

"Run!" The girls panicked.

Hundreds of black eagles were chasing them. The large birds flew above their heads and followed them; their claws were ready to grab them.

Good for the girls that Bruce and the boys were in excellent shape. They would not find it too difficult to run in order to get away. At at the same time, to carry the girls on their backs.

***

The women were looking behind them to see if the eagles were too close and if they could reach them. During their marathon, they realized there was nothing to protect them, nothing to provide them safety.

The sun hid for a while behind the clouds. They believed that the eagles were above them, ready to grab their exhausted bodies. A little bit later, rain decided to take over, but the eagles were still there and didn't stop chasing them.

After several minutes and after having a great distance from the initial spot, they saw something at the end of the black, brutal valley.

"What is that?" Lilly wasn't sure what to guess.

"I have no idea." Alicia rolled her eyes and prayed to God to save them.

"We should go there now!" Brittany trusted her instincts.

Only Brittany and the girls talked. It was unfeasible for the men to say a word; they were almost ready to faint. Their sweat was dripping onto the ground, and the only way to terminate this testing was to go inside the place in front of them.

"They are coming closer, Bruce!" Brittany paralyzed in fear.

No answer was heard. The brave men were doing their best to reach the place and, finally, they made it.

"Let's open the gate!" Bruce was acting like a maniac.

"How can we do that?" Dylan was trying to help him.

"I don't know, but we have to do it." Bruce was looking for a solution.

"Bruce, just breathe, you too, boys, don't talk too much." Brittany worried about them.

They were standing in front of the wooden gate of a weird building. Its structure was admirable. The rock solid fences that separated the whole building from the valley were amazing. Outside, it was all made of marble while the big sign above the main gate didn't distract them. They were absorbed in their determination to get into that place and escape the huge, black eagles coming for them. None of them could release the image of the claws ready to tear apart their flesh. It was a very difficult moment. The next few seconds would be critical for all of them.

"We need your help, girls; we can't open the gate

alone." Bruce was determined to save them all.

"Everybody push!" Dylan was ready to faint.

"We can't!" Lilly kept screaming.

"Push again!" Bruce was sure they would survive.

The last moment they managed to open the gate, leaving the eagles outside.

***

"No!!!" Brittany was next to Lilly.

"Everything is fine, Lilly." Lilly was breathing very fast.

Lilly woke up and realized that the beginning of their nightmare belonged to the past. Brittany was stroking her hair while she was trying to find out where they were this time.

Bruce waved at them and smiled. He could see the pavilion.

END

Trapped in Timelessness

Part Two:

Lake's Curse

By A.A Schenna

Dedication
To my family, the best present God has given me so far.

Chapter One

"We shouldn't be here." The young girl caressed Jason's face, her tone worried.

The moonlight, the smell of the trees and the beauty of the entire place had managed to seduce their minds.

The atmosphere started becoming more erotic. The heat and the thirst of their bodies triggered their desires. They loved discovering the first leaps of love.

"I want to be with you, Ciara."

"My parents will kill me. I should be home right now." Ciara gazed at Jason and smiled.

"Stay with me." Jason loved having his girlfriend with him.

"I can't, I have to go home."

"One last kiss," Jason hinted.

The beautiful teenage girl smiled and held his hand. She bit her lips and then kissed her boyfriend. Ciara was crazy in love with Jason. She loved knowing that all the students were talking about them. She always dreamed of being a famous person.

"I think I heard something." Ciara sounded serious.

"There's-no one else here." Jason tried to calm her.

"It's too late. We shouldn't be here," Ciara repeated, stepping back.

"Don't tell me that you are afraid of the dark." Jason started laughing.

"There's nothing here and we are in the middle of nowhere. And I don't like this lake." Ciara didn't like Jason's reaction either.

He started laughing. "Take it easy, baby, we are in Green Lake! We live in the most boring town of the world."

Ciara wanted to leave.

"It's our last year in this town; I look forward to

going to college," she murmured.

"It's just a year, baby, be patient." Jason took his girlfriend in his arms again and caressed her back.

"Can we go now?" Ciara couldn't stand being there one more minute.

"Okay."

They took a few steps. They heard the strange noise again and froze in fear. Ciara looked at Jason and held him tight. Jason remained silent and gazed upon the towering trees. The teenage boy waited to see the cause of the weird disturbance.

"What's happening?" Ciara whispered.

Out of the blue, the night birds began screaming like fatally wounded beasts.

"I am scared to death." Ciara locked her eyes on Jason. She wasn't strong enough to deal with the fear of the dark. She needed a hug. Ciara wanted to hear that everything would be fine.

The birds flew higher and, before long, hid behind the hill. The chilling noise disappeared.

"I want to go home," Ciara said impatiently.

Jason looked up at the sky and took a deep breath. He liked summer and the first hot days made him seek for the carefree memories of the previous summer.

Although he loved being there with Ciara, he had a bad feeling.

"It's over, baby, everything will be fine. I can't hear anything." He was lying but Ciara didn't realize it.

They walked to the dark path and when they saw the car, they decided to run. Jason's car was just a few meters away.

"What was that?" Ciara stopped, startled by a noise.

"I have no idea, baby." Jason didn't move.

"What..." Ciara couldn't breathe. When she saw the huge man standing behind her boyfriend, she froze in fear. That moment, Ciara realized they wouldn't escape.

"Jason!" she cried.

"Ciara, run!" The huge, naked man broke Jason's neck and then ran toward the teenage girl.

Ciara panicked. She started screaming and rushed to get in the car, her boyfriend's killer was faster and stronger.

The teenage girl didn't make it. She begged him for mercy, but he didn't even listen to her.

The following minutes nothing could be heard. Their bodies were lying on the rough ground while the night birds came back at the cursed area.

***

The tall, muscular man pulled his long hair away from his wild looking face and stood under the moonlight. He focused his sight on the surface of his timeless prison and he carried on staring at the guards of the curse. His black hair covered his back and the strange sign on his naked skin.

The soulless bodies of the residents of the small town were lying in the mud, as the blood kept falling in the cold water of the lake.

The lone cypresses which surrounded the silent place had managed to hide his presence while the night birds, the guards of the curse, continued flying above the corpses he had gathered.

He stretched out his strong arms and then he started dragging the lifeless bodies with a long, muddy rope into the lake.

He howled like a wild beast as his head moved up. Soon, the monster disappeared into the cold waters of the lake.

Before long, Jason and Ciara were gone too. Their soulless bodies disappeared into the cold water.

Chapter Two

"Leona, wake up! We have to go."

"I'm coming, Mom." Leona rolled her eyes and the memories of the past came up. *"I miss you so much,"* she whispered.

Seven months had passed since she had lost her father. Her fingers slipped on her father's photograph above her white desk, while the tears of his loss kept running down her face.

"Leona!" Her mother wanted to make sure she was ready.

"I'm coming!"

The beautiful girl swept the tears away and closed the door of the pink bedroom behind her.

"It's your last day at school and your brother is coming tonight! Now smile for me!"

"No photographs, Mom, please…in case you forgot, I am eighteen." Leona hated this part. She hated having her picture taken.

"But your father…" Both Leona and her mother fell silent.

The young woman walked to the door of the large kitchen and rested her sight on the lake. The view was incredible. The towering trees and the colors of the nature could steal everybody's attention.

"When is Brad coming home?" Leona couldn't stand the silence. She had to say something.

"I guess we'll see him tonight." Her mother sounded impatient.

Leona turned back and gazed at her mother. When she saw her eyes, she felt horrible. Leona realized her mother would never accept the truth.

She placed her cup of coffee on the table and sat down. She closed her eyes and wondered about destiny. *"Your father will no longer be with us."* Leona could still remember her mother's words.

Heart attack, yes, that's what the doctors said when Leona's mother left the school to go to the hospital. Two words, enough to kill Tracy Goodan. And that day, the charming teacher lost herself. She would never heal from that injury.

"Any plans after the school?" Leona's mother tried to sound normal.

"There's a party at the lake." She tried to sound like she was looking forward to it.

Tracy brushed her daughter's black hair away from her blue eyes and, that moment, Leona noticed the wrinkles on her mother's face. She was taken aback. Her mother looked different--she looked old. In just a few months, Tracy's glow was gone. The middle-aged woman had lost her beauty.

"That's great. I will be able to keep my eye on you." Tracy shook her head and smiled.

"We're late, Mom…"

Leona stood anxiously in front of the white door; she couldn't keep up living with all that pain and the silent complaints about life and destiny.

The teenage girl put her black bag on her back and waited for her mother.

"Okay, I was kidding," Tracy said, with a little laugh.

***

Tracy got out of the car and walked toward the beautiful, large yard. Soon, her blue eyes began searching for her daughter. When she saw Leona, she waved her hand. "I love you so much," she whispered.

Tracy felt the air of relief covering her sweaty face. She smiled at her daughter again and then placed her bag on the yellow chair under the brown pergola. She glanced at the towering cypresses and recalled the happy moments of the past.

"Where are you?" she asked. Tracy kept wondering about life and the secrets of destiny. She missed her husband, she missed her son, and she missed her family. "You had no right to leave me alone," she said. "How am I supposed to protect our kids, I need you..." she confessed.

Tracy sat in the chair, thinking of her husband. The wonderful moments they had shared at the paradise in front of her haunted her mind. Tracy would never forget the moments they were chasing their children around their house. She would never forget the times they were all sitting in front of the fireplace when it snowed.

Tracy stood up and got into the house. A few minutes later she came back outside and put the bottle of the red wine on the small table. She swallowed the tranquilizers and she closed her eyes. She hated doing that, but there was no other way. The pain in her soul insisted on killing all of her hopes.

Chapter Three

"Where are Jason and Ciara?" Leona asked.
"I have no idea Leona; I guess they're out having fun." The speaker bit her tongue.
"Mary…" Leona laughed.

The young woman looked around her and felt peaceful. Everybody was having fun in the most beautiful place of the small town. The huge trees which surrounded the lake made her feel lost in paradise.

"Your boyfriend is coming and I saw some friends over there." Mary waved at the blonde boy with the blue eyes and left her friend alone.

"Okay." Leona looked behind her and realized that all the girls were hooked by his presence. That moment she felt weird, she was jealous.

Nick had always been there for her. He would do anything for Leona.

"Hi baby." The tall, well-shaped teenager hugged Leona and smelled her perfume.

"Hi." Leona seemed anxious.

"Is everything okay?" Nick remained stable.

"I don't see Jason and Ciara. Have you?"

"No, I haven't, but I am sure they are hiding somewhere." Nick's expression made her smile.

"Stop it." Leona burrowed against him and laughed.

"I am so happy to see you smiling again." Nick was crazy in love with his girlfriend.

"I know. I owe this to you." Leona was ready to cry.

"I am sorry, baby." Nick sounded serious.

"What do you mean? I don't understand." Leona fixed her eyes on him.

"You will understand." Nick lifted her up and ran toward the lake.

"No, Nick!"

They fell into the cold water and the rest of the

students followed them, shrieking with delight. The many beers and the music added to the party atmosphere. Everybody was seeking for a crazy adventure. They were all celebrating the arrival of summer.

"You are crazy." Leona hugged Nick and kissed him.

"I love you, Leona." The moment her eyes pierced his, she was sure that Nick would never betray her.

It was the first time after a long period Leona felt happy. The last months, the teenage girl was living a hell. Now, she was ready to move on. Leona believed that the worst part was over.

"I love you too, Nick."

The young couple got out of the water while their friends carried on carousing and drinking beers. Leona took off her bright blue jeans and Nick couldn't stop looking at her black swimsuit. The beautiful girl smiled and helped him take off his white T-shirt.

"What are you looking at?" she asked.

"Your eyes…?" Nick didn't know what to say.

They stayed in the sun and continued having fun together. They were in love. There was no doubt about that.

"Will you be by my side forever?" Leona's insecurities came up.

"I will never leave you." Nick meant his words. He really did.

***

"Mom?" Leona ran to her mother's side and Nick followed her.

"What is it?" Tracy asked vaguely, having no idea where she was.

"Are you okay?" Leona knelt and held her mother's head. Tracy was sleeping on the brown tile floor.

"Yea… where is your brother?" She was trying to pull herself back together.

"I don't know." Leona was struggling not to expose

59

her dismay.

"What time is it, how about the party?" Tracy tried to stand up but it was impossible. She couldn't move.

"It's too late and the party is over."

Leona turned back and gazed at Nick. "I'll see you tomorrow," she said.

"Let me help you."

"I can do this." Leona rolled her eyes and took a deep breath.

"I know you can do it, just let me help you." Nick placed his hand on her back and waited for her answer.

"I'll call you later." Nick nodded and left the house.

"Okay, it's just you and me now, Mom."

Tracy realized what had happened but it was too late to fix things. Leona was there and she knew. Her daughter had discovered her secret.

Tracy shook her head. "I'm sorry," she mumbled. With the lights shining on her face, she looked like a sorrowful angel.

"That's okay, Mom."

When Leona saw the tranquilizers and the bottle of the wine on the floor, she was taken aback. She had no idea about her mother's addiction. And she couldn't lose her too.

Leona wanted to scream. She just couldn't take it anymore.

Instead, she helped her mother lie on the bed and stayed with her until she fell asleep. Afterwards, she closed the door of the house behind her and lit a cigarette.

Leona swept the tears from her face and walked toward the dark alley outside the house. The huge branches of the trees had managed to hide the road to her shelter. At night, the peaceful lake was her best friend. It was the only place where she could think without being distracted.

Chapter Four

T he moonlight didn't manage to steal her attention and take her anger away. Her sight remained locked on the peaceful surface of the water while, Leona's tears didn't stop running down her face. She had crossed the wooden bridge and now she was sitting on a huge rock in the middle of the lake.

Leona couldn't find a way to get past the nasty facts that had settled in her life. The despair continued surrounding her soul.

The young woman shook her head, rippling her long, black hair. She placed her elbows on her knees and she started thinking of her brother. She missed him so much. If only she had someone to support her and make her sure that things would get better.

Nick was always there for her, but he'd never learned what family meant. His parents dumped him when he was nine years old and his unwilling grandparents were forced to raise him. Nick had never run into love. He could never understand what she was going through.

Although the night was almost over, the towering trees were not willing to welcome the dawn and the daylight. Nevertheless, Leona was patient.

She was looking forward to seeing the sun. The sun's rays could help her gain back the strength she was missing to move on. The light could help her soul overcome the difficulties of life. She had done it before and, now, she would do it again.

The young woman looked up at the sky and seemed ready to come closer to the truth. Every time Leona felt unable to face up the difficulties of life, she used to stare up there to see if an angel could come down to earth to help her get away from everything.

At some point, she thought she heard someone walking to her side, and she decided to speak up.

"Who's there?" She stood up and looked around her. She could see nothing and no one. Soon enough, the dark covered her soul. Leona felt there was something terrible going on.

The moment she heard something crawling on the dry, rough ground, she panicked. Although Leona knew there were many animals living around the lake, she could bet there was something else that caused the strange, chilling noise she was hearing now. No one had ever warned the people who lived in the Green Lake about the existence of dangerous beasts.

"Who's there?" The chilling noise was coming closer to her ears.

Leona searched the place, but she found nothing other than some rocks to defend herself. That was the best she could do.

"Who's there?"

Big night birds began making circles above the lake. Leona gazed at them and wondered about their presence. She had never seen such birds before. There were ten white birds which looked like huge gulls. They frightened her.

"Leona?" Her boyfriend was searching for her.

Nick had decided to stand by her side. He didn't go home. He drove back at his girlfriend's house and, when he didn't find her home, he guessed where she would be.

He was the only one Leona was sure she could rely on.

The moment she turned her sight on the woods, his beastlike face was already in front of her, grabbing at her. She could feel his cold breath.

He had done his work, it was time to go, but he wouldn't lose the chance to trap everyone else in the timeless prison. He was the master of the lake. Everything surrounded by the water belonged to him. He had the power to do anything he wanted. He had the power to define the fate of his next victims.

"Oh my God! Nick, help me!" Leona pushed the monster away and tried to escape.

"I'm coming, Leona!" Nick could now see her. He threw the flashlight on his face and rushed to help his girlfriend.

The wild man grabbed Leona and bit her lips, a rough kiss. She froze in terror, unable to fight any longer. He turned and threw her into the water. The shock broke her paralysis.

With no fear, Nick stepped on the huge rock and stood in front of the monster. He started punching the wild man. But he couldn't hurt him. It was like fighting against a wall of concrete.

"I'll kill you!" Nick was out of control.

"Somebody, please help us!" Leona believed he would kill them.

The wild man placed his hands on Nick's neck and lifted him up. Then he bit his lips and threw Nick into the water and Leona rushed to him. Her boyfriend was bleeding and she tore a piece of fabric from the bottom of her shirt to staunch the flow.

"What do you want?" Nick cried. "Stay away!"

The personification of their worst nightmares disappeared under the water and resurfaced moments later towing a long, muddy rope. Nick and Leona, terrified, watched in silence.

When he started passed them, the rope trailing behind him, Nick and Leona held each other tight, unable to look away from the victims.

When Leona saw the long rope and the dead bodies, she threw up. She counted ten bodies and she recognized some of the dead people.

If only she knew their fate.

"Ten days, ten souls, every century," their attacker intoned.

"You belong to me and you'll wait for me till the next time."

The wild naked man kept looking at them until he dived in the water and disappeared. The strange birds, the long rope, and the dead were gone.

Nick and Leona, on the rock, turned toward the shore.

Chapter Five

"**B**rad! Welcome home, darling." Tracy looked fine. She was happy and seemed to have forgotten the previous night.

"Thanks Mom, it's nice to see you again." The young man left the newspaper on the table and stood up. He had missed the incredible view and his family. He looked forward to hugging his mother and sister again.

The handsome man held his mother tight while she kept caressing his black, curly hair.

"Where's your sister?" Tracy wasn't able to remember the details.

"I have no idea. Her cell phone is here." Brad showed her Leona's phone and, that moment, he found his mother's behavior strange.

"She must have slept at Kelly's house. Now tell me, how is college?" Tracy was acting as if nothing had happened.

"Everything's fine, Mom." Brad was puzzled about his mother's reaction. He sat down and began reading the newspaper, masking his concern for his mother and missing sister.

Brad knew his mother very well. He was sure she was pretending. In his eyes, Tracy looked exhausted and helpless. She could hardly move. Moreover, her attitude confirmed his suspicions about her addiction to alcohol and drugs.

"Okay, what are you reading?" Tracy wanted to talk with her son.

"The news." Brad didn't look at her. He decided to ignore his mother to make her realize her responsibilities. He hated acting like this way, but Tracy didn't give him another choice.

"Anything interesting?"

Tracy stood behind her son's back and kissed

Brad's head. It was her way of saying sorry. She wanted to apologize. She was looking for sympathy.

"As always." Brad turned back and stared at his mother. He smiled and she shook her head yes. She would change things.

"Read for me." His mother said.

"Four students along with their two teachers are still missing and we have the legend of the lake--"

"What lake?" Tracy sounded curious.

"The one which lies near our house, Mom," Brad said.

"Read the article for me."

"Mom..." Brad never liked reading articles concerning tales, traditions, and mystery.

"Please, honey." Tracy took her favorite white cup, filled it with coffee, and sat next to her son.

"Many centuries ago, a fatal disease had killed more than the half of a village which was covered by towering cypresses."

"They are talking about our town," Brad said.

"Yea, I know." Tracy wanted to hear everything.

"The Burning Tree, the tribal leader." The young man made a pause and looked at his mother.

"Now that's a beautiful name," he said.

"Brad!" Tracy smiled.

"The leader of the village, a Native American young man, called the four spirits of nature to make a deal to save the village and the lives of his people.

"When his raft reached the middle of the lake, the night birds notified the four spirits. He was scared to death, but he was determined to save his people.

"After many hours, they made a deal, but the terms were harsh. For ten days, every century, the leader of the village would have to deliver ten souls to the spirits of nature. For ten days, he would have the power to do anything, as long as he was in the lake. He could use the water to capture and trap his victims. He could exploit the power of the water.

"The Burning Tree" (the tradition mentions that, when he got angry, smoke covered his body and he looked like a tree which was on fire), had lost his family due to the fatal disease, and the only thing he was looking for was revenge. He was not able to think clearly. He had no idea how his decision would affect his spirit. He was not aware of the consequences of his choice.

"The wild man had lost his mind and had become obsessive with the presence of death. He was furious; he wanted to fight with death. He wanted to defeat death. But he had ignored the fact that he was human.

"Finally, he made the deal and the villagers, his people, survived. But his soul trapped in the lake, forever. He was transformed into a supernatural beast that had no feelings. He would always remain a slave. He would serve the spirits of nature forever."

"Oh, my God." Tracy felt sorry for him.

"And that was the story of our lake." Brad put the newspaper down and drank his coffee.

"That was a great story." Tracy looked outside at the lake.

"It's just fiction, a legend, Mom." Brad smiled.

"I know, honey" she whispered.

"I am going at Kelly's house to see if Leona is there." Brad stood up and so did his mother.

"Okay baby, I have to go to work, but I will see you both in the afternoon."

"Okay, have a great day." Brad got his car keys, and kissed his mom.

"You too, honey," she said.

Chapter Six

Nick and Leona were resting on the large rock, their feet in the cold water. They looked like castaways who were stranded on a small island surrounded by the sea.

Both had caught their breath, and stopped each other's bleeding. But the consequences of their battle against the curse were not over yet.

"I think we should go home," Leona said. There was nothing she wanted more.

"You're right." Nick was ready.

"What are we going to tell my mom?" Leona glanced toward her boyfriend.

Nick gave no answer. "Let's go home," he said.

Nick stood up and helped Leona up. He held her hand, smiled reassuringly at her, and they headed for the wooden bridge.

Although it was a hot day, they sensed the cold water on their skin--which covered their ankles—would not release them. The water had become another obstacle during their getaway. They couldn't get out of the lake.

"What is it?" Leona asked.

"I don't know." Nick sounded anxious, looking at the bridge.

"Why did you stop?" Leona was tired and she also missed her bed. She had no idea what was happening.

"I can't move." Nick was scared.

"What do you mean?" She tried to move on, but she was stopped in her tracks.

"It's like there's a wall between the lake and the land. We can't step out of the water." Nick was sure he was right.

"Oh my God..." Leona sealed her mouth and locked her eyes on him.

"I don't understand," Nick said, trying again and

again.

"There must be something we can do to get out of this place." Leona cried out.

***

The following hours they did everything to escape, but their efforts had no result. Everything was in vain. They were tired, sleepless and, in addition, they should have been at school. The graduation had come. The students had arranged a big party.

"What is happening?" Leona had so many questions.

"I have no idea." Nick was helpless.

They didn't stop calling for help. They did everything they could imagine to steal somebody's attention but nothing. It was like no one could see or hear them.

"I want to go home." Leona was desperate.

"Me too, Leona."

"My house is right there, you can see it!"

"I know that, Leona."

"Then why can't we get out of the lake?"

"You should better get used to that," Nick said. He sounded resigned.

"What do you mean?" Leona suspected what he was about to say, but didn't want to hear it.

"When he bit me, I saw some weird things. We are trapped in this lake," Nick said, meeting her eyes. "We can't leave."

"Are you insane?" Leona asked angrily.

"You've got to face up the truth."

"I will get us out of here. I'll figure it out. I don't care how long it takes."

"I really hope you'll make it." Nick kept gazing at Leona.

No matter what, he loved seeing her not giving up. He admired her strength.

69

Chapter Seven

Tracy gazed at the small children playing in the water and smiled. She loved watching them. Somehow, she was jealous of them. She missed the old times when she had nothing to worry about.

If only Tracy could get these feelings and personal memories back.

Lucky you, she thought.

The tired teacher took off her sunglasses and placed them in the pocket of her green shirt. She went in the house and found a distraught Brad.

"Leona is missing." Brad couldn't stop moving around the living room.

"What? Did you talk with her friends? Did you go to the police?" Tracy asked. She put her bag on the couch and paid attention to her son's words.

"I did all those you said. As far as the police alert is concerned, we have to wait for forty-eight hours. Until then, Leona is not officially a missing person."

Tracy picked up her bag again and moved toward the door.

"Where are you going?" Brad didn't know what she was doing.

"I'm going to find my daughter."

Once she left, Brad went to Leona's bedroom to see if there were any signs of where she had gotten to.

***

The sunset was gone when the stars started making their appearance in the beautiful sky. Leona and Nick were lying on the huge rock, thinking of their futures. Their eyes were locked on the wooden bridge. They had crossed that bridge so many times in the past.

"What are we going to do?" Leona asked.

"I guess we can do nothing. We have to accept

reality." Nick was not thinking of the past. He could live without memories.

"What about our families?" Leona whispered.

"I don't have a family. My parents and my grandparents hated me. It's better this way, for all of us. At least, I am here with you."

His girlfriend smiled and lay against him.

They remembered the times they were counting the stars and, somehow, they forgot their situation. They were tired and sleepless, but they wanted to stay connected to the good days from the past as well.

***

Tracy had searched the entire area around the lake. Tracy didn't stop calling her daughter's name. She had searched for eight hours straight, determined to find her daughter.

In the meantime, an exhausted Brad was searching for his sister in the small town. The hunt only brought him failure after failure.

"Where are you, Leona?" he whispered.

Besides his mother, Brad realized that his sister needed someone to support her as well. Leona had no one to express the pain she felt.

Where could she be? Brad kept wondering.

***

Tracy was trying to remember Leona's hiding places, and recalled the times she caught Leona smoking her father's cigarettes.

She set off for the lake again. The sun was gone and the night had dressed the whole area.

Tracy hoped she would see Leona at the wooden bridge, but no one was there.

"What's happening?" Leona woke up and looked up at the bridge, hearing footsteps.

"Your mother," Nick said and Leona rushed toward her, only to be repelled.

71

"I am so sorry, Mom!" Leona cried.

The woman crossed the short bridge and walked toward the huge, grey rock while wondering about her daughter's behavior.

"Leona had no reason to leave home," she mumbled. Yes, she was certain about that.

"I am really sorry, Mom." Leona's tears ran down her pale cheeks.

The hopeless mother gazed at the body of the peaceful lake and, a couple of minutes later, she used the flashlight to check out the surface of the rock. She wanted to see if there were any cigarettes.

"I will never hurt you again, Mom." Leona reached out to hug her mother but couldn't touch her.

"Where are you, Leona?" Tracy cried out.

"I'm here, Mom." Leona was ready to collapse.

Tracy heard a strange noise and she turned back.

"Who's there?" Tracy asked.

"It's me." Brad crossed the bridge and stood next to his mother.

"Did you find your sister?" Tracy was shaking. She wished he would say yes.

"No, I didn't." Brad shook his head.

"What are you doing? I am here! What kind of joke is this?" Leona couldn't understand what was happening. She was in front of them but they couldn't see her. They couldn't hear her voice and they couldn't touch her body.

When Leona stared at Nick, he tried to hide his tears. Nick knew.

"I made her leave the house, Brad. I was a bad mother." Tracy blamed herself for her daughter's reaction.

"No Mom, you were perfect, you did nothing wrong." Leona was shocked. Once more she tried to touch her mother but she didn't make it. She couldn't feel her heartbeat.

"Let's go home. We need some rest. We'll eat

something and then we will come back to search for Leona." Brad hugged his mother and helped her walk toward their house.

"I am here, we are here, don't leave us!" Leona was screaming but they could hear nothing. Leona was scared to death.

"Are we dead, Nick?" Leona asked.

"I'm not sure, baby," he answered.

***

The sound of something heavy being dragged along the rough ground startled Tracy. The sweat kept running down her face and soaked her pillows. She was used to having nightmares, but this one was completely different.

She turned the flashlight on the hill and saw a naked woman dragging a dead body with a long, muddy rope.

"Oh my God..."

Tracy lost her balance, stumbled over a big rock, and fell into the water. The moment she stood up, the woman was in front of her face.

"Leona..." she whispered, still sleeping.

Her daughter didn't say a word. Leona was not even breathing. The girl with the amazing beauty was no longer her child. Her blue eyes had turned black. Her skin was cold, it was dead.

"My precious baby..."

Tracy tried to place her hands on her daughter's face, but she didn't make it. Leona had already dragged the dead body in the water. She had disappeared. Tracy was there alone.

"Your daughter will be fine." She turned back but she couldn't see anyone.

"Who are you?" Tracy whispered.

"Leona is an Alpha; the beast will never get her."

"I want her back!" she screamed.

"You still have your son." Tracy opened her eyes and stared at the white ceiling.

73

"It's just a dream, just a dream." Tracy swept the sweat from her face and drank some water.

The frightened woman realized that she would never see her daughter again.

"Come back, Leona."

"What is it?" Brad stood by his mother and held her hands.

"Leona won't come back." Tracy sounded certain.

"What are you saying?" Brad didn't believe her words.

"Something weird must have happened. I saw her in the lake. Your sister left us forever. Her soul is in the middle of life and death. She isn't even human anymore." Tracy had no doubt. The voice she heard helped her accept the truth. She knew that Leona was safe, but that she'd never see her daughter again.

"We will find her," Brad said.

"No, we will not."

Chapter Eight

"Grandma, you always sit outside looking at the lake! Come in the house."

"I'm coming, Leona." Tracy glanced upon her granddaughter and smiled.

Thirty years later, Tracy couldn't take her eyes off the lake. She knew she would never have the chance to meet her daughter again. She was almost eighty years old.

Tracy never stopped thinking of Leona. Police never found her body. They never found Nick as well. But Tracy knew what had happened.

As time passed by, the anger, the despair, and the thirst for revenge had stolen Tracy's thoughts.

"Are you coming?" Tracy was still looking at the lake.

She couldn't help watching the lake which had trapped her daughter's soul.

Chapter Nine

Leona and Nick were not affected by the time. They remained ageless but trapped in the lake and, after a small period, they decided to stop hoping they would escape from the timeless prison they were locked in.

As time passed by, both the young woman and her partner lost almost all of their physical needs. But the attraction was still there.

They both gained powers they could never imagine. They were not humans anymore. They had become two supernatural beings.

During the daylight hours, they could walk on the surface of the water, while during the nights they could fly. But, even though they were powerful, they couldn't escape from the body of the lake.

"I haven't seen my mom lately," Leona said.

"I'm sure she is fine." Nick smiled at her and she went closer to his side.

"What happened to us, Nick? Why are we here?" Leona would never adjust to this way of life.

"Do you remember the last days of our lives as they used to be?"

"Yes, I do." Leona sounded curious.

"Everybody was talking about something strange. Out of the blue, two teachers along with four students vanished, and no one could explain what had happened to them." His eyes locked on hers.

"What's your point?" Leona seemed to be interested.

"I had heard a scientist talking about being trapped in timelessness. Somehow, we are trapped in timelessness."

"This is crazy." Leona started laughing.

"No, it's not." Nick sounded angry.

"Yes, it is," his girlfriend said.

***

76

"What happened?" she asked.

"You passed out."

The teenaged girl rolled her eyes and leaned against the tree. She could smell the leaves and the ground.

"Where are we?" She asked again.

"We're back home." The brunette woman helped her stand up.

When they reached the rest of the company up there, they all felt lucky. They loved the view.

"There are some houses over there," the young man shouted as he pointed at the beautiful town.

"I can see them!" his partner confessed.

They walked through the path and, a few meters further, they gazed at a black, convertible car.

"I like it," the teenage boy whispered.

The older man bent at his knees and noticed the blood on the ground. He also saw the silver bracelet. In a flash he took it and put it in the pocket of his pants.

"Let's go," he said.

***

"What is it?" Leona couldn't stand seeing him distant.

"I am fine, baby." Nick hadn't changed at all.

"Oh my God…" Leona was taken aback.

"What happened?" Nick didn't even look at his girlfriend.

"Look over there." Leona pointed at the people.

There were four teenagers walking toward the lake while, a few meters behind them, a man and a woman in their mid-thirties followed, looking around them. The two boys and the two girls must have been around fifteen to seventeen years old.

Their cloths looked dirty as they came closer to Nick and Leona, and they seemed nervous. They were enthralled by the presence of the first people they'd seen since their adventures and battles with the beasts, the scorpions, and the monsters.

Without a rational explanation, they all felt they belonged to the same team.

"Don't think about it, baby; it's time to get over it." Nick had lost hope.

"I think…" Leona felt weird. When she gazed at the teenagers, she sensed their agony. She could feel whatever they felt. There was a strange connection with these people.

"Hello there!" the oldest man said in a friendly voice. Although he knew there was something crazy going on, he didn't want to scare these kids and of course the other members of his company.

There were no words to describe Nick and Leona's joy. After thirty years, someone could see them again.

Nick stood up and held Leona's hand. It was the first time that his smile came back on his face.

"Hi." The young man crossed the bridge and stretched out his arm. "I'm Bruce."

"I'm Nick and this is my girlfriend, Leona."

"Nice to meet you kids. Over there you can see Brittany, Lilly, Alicia, Dylan, and Jack." Nick and Leona waved and smiled at them.

"It's a miracle," Leona whispered.

"I don't understand." Bruce was still confused.

"Pull us out, please." Leona locked her gaze on his eyes. She saw everything they had gone through. She could steal his memories. She could understand if someone was a good or a bad person.

"What do you mean?" Bruce had no idea what she meant.

"Let me show you."

The three walked towards shore, Bruce on the bridge, Nick and Leona on the lake. Bruce stepped off the bridge. Leona stretched out her arm, offering her hand. Nick did the same thing.

"Pull us out."

Bruce took their hands and pulled them ashore. "You did it! You set us free! Thank you!"

The rest of company continued looking at the young couple. "I am going home." Leona ran toward her house and the rest followed her steps. She was thrilled.

Chapter Ten

Leona reached her house and rang the bell. The rest stood behind her and waited for someone to open the door.

"Come on!" Leona knocked at the door. She looked forward to seeing her mother again.

"I'm coming."

When they saw the woman who opened the door, Leona was fighting back tears. She bit her lips and shook her head.

"Stupid kids," the woman said, and closed the door in their faces.

"She can't see us!" Leona cried.

When the despairing girl looked back, everybody was petrified.

She walked to the table and grabbed the newspaper. When she mentioned the date she read, everyone froze in fear.

Bruce was looking at Brittany, his partner, his prop, wondering about the entire situation. Lilly and Alicia kept staring at Dylan and Jack. Nick carried on shaking his head no.

"We've been there for more than thirty years, Nick. My mom might be dead," Leona whispered.

"I don't know what to say, baby," Nick said.

"Who are you?" Leona asked the group.

"I want to know the same thing too, young lady." Brittany stood in front of the daring girl and seemed nervous.

Everything had changed. No one was supposed to live like a ghost.

"We are eight people. Two people are still missing. When they'll find us, we will know everything." Everyone stared at him.

"How do you know that?" Bruce asked.

"I had some weird dreams. I can't tell you anything else because I don't know anything other than that." Nick would never hide the truth, especially from Leona.

The entire situation was so complicated that they didn't know how to react. They had to wait. They had to be patient.

A few minutes later, they left Leona's house and headed to the forest. They had to calm down and think of their future.

Bruce sat down on the ground and kept looking at the kids who stared at the lake. They were all silent and scared. They were petrified but they felt lucky since they had one another. They were a team.

Under other circumstances, this would be a perfect summer day since the beauty of the place was flirting intensely with the serenity they were looking for. But, now, they were still fighting against the insecurities and consequences of an absurd fate.

***

Sara and Rick looked helpless. The young couple swam toward the shore. They were stranded in the middle of the lake and they wanted to get out of the cold water. They were determined to survive.

"They are here," Nick said and looked at the rest.

"I see them." Leona pointed at the lake and then nodded at Brittany.

"Let's find out what's happening." Bruce gazed upon Brittany and held her hand. The moment he stood in front of her face, he smiled and squeezed her palm. She was his beloved partner. And he was sure that things would get better.

They all ran toward the coast to help the two people. Bruce and Brittany were hooked by their facial expressions. It was obvious that Rick and Sara were scared to death and they needed support. The blood on their clothes and the bruises on their faces made the rest of the team feel ready to fight for them.

"Please help us." Sara sounded hopeless.

Lilly, Alicia, Dylan, and Jack rushed to get them out of the water while Bruce and Brittany tried to calm them.

"Everything will be fine," Brittany said.

Nick and Leona were taken aback. They couldn't explain what was happening.

"What's your name?" Bruce asked.

"I'm Rick and this is my wife Sara." The young man hugged his partner and, immediately, she felt safe. They had managed to escape. They could still breathe and that was amazing. The mud had wrapped up their bodies, but they were still alive. And they were circled by a team they had no idea they were part of.

"I'm Bruce. This is Brittany, Lilly, Alicia, Dylan Jack, Nick, and Leona." He smiled and so did Rick and Sara.

"Nice to meet you." Rick was curious about everything, but he was patient as well.

Suddenly Sara pointed at the sky and everyone looked up at the white clouds. They could all see a man flying. They had no idea where he came from and were curious about his ability as well. He had no wings and he didn't move his hands.

"Oh my God! Who is this man? What is he doing?" Sara was surprised.

No one answered her questions. They were all staring at him.

Now, the aged man seemed like walking in the air. His white attire and his facial expression made them feel peaceful while Bruce, Brittany and their four students smiled. They had missed his company. They looked forward to seeing a friend.

"Hi Marc," Bruce said.

The aged man smiled and observed the rest four people.

"I see you are all here," Marc whispered.

"What's happening? Bruce asked.

They heard a terrible sound, a huge explosion. Smoke and ash covered the sky and a horrible sound of countless people screaming and calling for help assailed their ears. They could see nothing, but the terrifying noise completely surrounded them.

"You are an Alpha, Bruce, like all of you here." Marc gazed at them, but no one could understand what he was trying to say.

"What does this mean?" Brittany asked nervously.

"Humanity is in great danger. The demons will kill all human beings. Your mission is to protect them." Marc placed his hands on Bruce's shoulders and locked his eyes on his.

"How are we supposed to do that? We are human beings too," Bruce whispered.

"No, you are not. You are all supernatural beings." Marc sounded proud of them.

"What do you mean?" Bruce asked again.

"You are immortal and powerful. Very soon you will be able to realize your strength," Marc said.

"What do we have to do?" Bruce asked.

"I will tell you everything you need to know," Marc said.

Marc told them about the future and their mission. They were all surprised, but impatient as well. They wanted to know everything. They wanted to help those who needed protection.

The good days belonged to the past. The carefree moments would remain a sweet memory which would help them overcome the daily problems.

People around the world had never thought they would see the final destruction. Those who had managed to survive would have to struggle to defeat the challenges of life.

Finding food, water, and shelter would become the goal of each day for the rest of their lives.

The demons were back and angrier than ever before. They were determined to destroy everyone on earth. No one could fight against them except the Alphas.

Trapped in Timelessness

The Alphas

By A.A Schenna

Dedication

To my family and Maria, the best presents God has given me so far, and to readers all around the world.

Dark Secrets
656 BC

"**Y**ou destroyed everything!" The tall man was exclaimed, trying to unchain his hands.

"No, you destroyed us," the powerful speaker, the winner of this battle answered and looked at his enemy, feeling sorry for him.

"We could be together in this. We could do anything, Marc." He couldn't accept his failure and forthcoming punishment as he attempted to earn Marc's trust by making him feel emotionally trapped.

"It's over, Leonim." Marc would never disrespect the law.

"I will never forget your betrayal, Marc. The next time I will kill your Alphas after cutting off your head first." Leonim was sure he would be given another chance, and didn't hesitate to threaten the leader of white soldiers of their lord as well.

"You will miss being embodied, Leonim. I will see you the final day again." Marc waved his left hand at the guards and took him away while he watched his violent removal in silence.

"You will regret it, Marc. I will kill you and your Alphas like you did to my race," Marc shouted out, scuffing his feet roughly on the ground, trapping the white soldiers in a cloud of dust. He was unable to accept the consequences of his mutiny and kept resisting.

Marc turned back and walked to the place where the first Alphas had been slaughtered by Leonim and the rest of the revolutionists. The moment he gazed at their bleeding, soulless bodies, he cried out and, although he was aware of how things would evolve, he could do nothing but admire their strength. He had truly loved these people and never stopped admiring their passion to protect their offspring by sacrificing their lives.

Marc made a circle around the place they were found and, later, he knelt in front of the true fighters, touching their bodies while praying for their souls before giving the final signal to burn the temples of their pure hearts.

"The gates are closed. Leonim and the rest will remain locked in until the last day. The offspring of the first Alphas are enough to restart everything again," the tall man opposite him intoned.

The white angel got up and remained stable, staring for the last time at the first Alphas. The dark had covered the forest and the towering oak trees--the last remaining paradise on earth-- but the new day would turn into the new beginning of humanity.

After a while, the fire turned the bodies of the first Alphas into ash whereas the smoke kept rising, becoming one with the white clouds of euphoria, seeking for a shelter to transfer and let their souls rest in peace.

The black angels were defeated and now they would remain trapped in the abyss, the zone between life and death, unable to do anything other than wait for their punishment.

"I think we are done here," Marc said and looked toward his powerful soldiers. The white angels nodded at their leader and waited for his next move.

Marc looked around him and spread his great wings to take to the air. The rest of his team followed him back. Flying higher, Marc remembered the past and his initial reaction, considering whether he could have done something to prevent this from happening or not.

***

"Look at them!" Leonim said contemptuously.

"It's not our business." Marc said firmly.

"The only thing they know is producing offspring, they are pathetic," Leonim added, pointing at the people who lived in small villages. Some were enjoying lovely intimate moments.

"You know the rules, Leonim." Marc was able to guess Leonim's thoughts.

"We could make things different, Marc. We could be their Gods and worship both of us everyday." Leonim whispered, feeling guilty for his selfish confession.

"Are you insane?" Marc shook his head, trying to forget his words.

"Stand by my side and I will help you do everything you want," Leonim dared to suggest while Marc remained speechless, coming across the ruthless reality.

"I will pretend you never said that, Leonim." Marc murmured.

"I understand."

That moment Marc realized that his brother had lost his mind, desiring the privilege of their father. He was certain that nothing would be the same again since Leonim stepped into the zone of selfishness, ignoring the law and disregarding the love of their father. Leonim regarded that he could make everything better whereas nothing and no one would be able to stop him.

The following day, Marc found Leonim sleeping with the daughter of a man under the shadow of an oak tree. He loved his brother, and now froze in fear because he knew what their father would do to him.

"What have you done?" Marc cried, trying to hide his tears. Leonim had crossed the line and betrayed them all.

"I decided to change everything and make a new race. Come with me, Marc, we could be the best team. Our offspring will become very strong--no one will be able to hurt them and we will become their Gods." Leonim was so passionate with his plan that he couldn't understand the consequences of his actions yet.

"You did something you knew was forbidden," Marc whispered.

"I will make my own world, my own race." Leonim didn't have the least of intention of seeing their father, begging for mercy.

"I am sorry for you." Marc stepped back and disappeared into the sky, tormented by his brother's actions.

***

Before long, everything changed. The balance was destroyed and the rules were broken. The first generations of the human beings came across despair and hard times since the battle between the white and the black angels lasted for too long, making the people suffer until, finally, the white angels threw the black angels on earth where they destroyed everything.

The black angels killed the men and burned everything except their territory while they kept the women to make the new race. The embodied dark spirits turned the beauty of the earth into a living hell as the ash and the smoke covered the air, the four seas, and the sky. When they rushed to kill the offspring of the first human beings, the Alphas were scared to death. They would do anything to protect their children.

The white angels decided to intervene since the first Alphas were not strong enough to defeat the black angels and the power of the dark. They managed to save their children. But they would never become special like their ancestors.

The next Alphas wouldn't have the same luck since they would have the power to avoid them, feeling confident in a world without safety.

Marc would guide them to the paths of hell and black magic, explaining everything.

The two teachers, Bruce, Brittany and his students Jack, Dylan, Lilly Alicia along with Leona, Nick, Sara, and Rick would become the first Alphas with limitless power.

Shortly After The Final Appearance Of The Black Angels
Minnesota, U.S.
Nowadays

I never thought I would live like a wild beast. The moment I heard the rest of our team screaming while searching for something to eat, I froze, paralyzed in fear and disgust.

I rested my hands on the rough ground and squeezed the black sand with my dirty, skinny fingers. I thought the whole situation was tragic, it was insane; no one was supposed to live like that.

I looked up at the sky and already knew I would be disappointed again. I was looking forward to seeing the sun but, for once more, I came across vanity and despair.

The blue color had vanished as the dust had covered everything and, during the night, you could see no clouds, no stars, not even the moon.

The strange fog along with the ash carried on wrapping the whole place up. Then again, the grey and the black colors had settled in front of my eyes and, as far as I could tell, they would remain there forever.

Although the intense heat belonged to the past, I was sure that we hadn't seen anything yet. Soon, the weather conditions would change and the lack of sunlight would cause us more problems, making our living more difficult.

I swept my face and felt my dry eyes ready to pop out and, while I kept looking around me, the picture was still the same. I could sense the dangerous silence and, at the same time, I couldn't explain how we managed to land at zero, destroying everything we had achieved.

Out of the blue, most of the world's population was gone--assuming due to a tragic sun explosion. We were the only people who were still alive, and while we could still breathe, we were all cursed to exist. If only we could live again.

Unfortunately, all of us who survived were condemned to keep up living in a hell, and even though we were not zombies or man-eaters, I could bet that our hunger would be able to turn us into something we were not.

I gazed at my new "family" and rolled my eyes. After a while I leaned against the wrecks of modern's life destruction and tried to recall my life before the "new world."

The moment I sensed her presence, my eyes pierced hers and I smiled since I realized that I hadn't lost everything yet. She sat down next to me and held my hand, looking into my eyes while seeking for a place to rest her soul. We still had one another and we were both grateful for that precious privilege.

The black back seat of a destroyed jeep had become our bed and we felt lucky about that since there was nothing else around us to remind us of the positive pictures of the past.

Nevertheless, we had to be patient and optimistic since we were stranded in a place where everything seemed willing to eat avidly the last thing we had. We struggled to keep it alive, our precious, wonderful thoughts from before.

***

"It's Sunday, wake up!" I looked upon my wife and smiled.

I was definitely the luckiest man on earth; I always thought that Alyson was the most beautiful woman I had ever seen.

"Michael..." my wife murmured.

"I am coming." I would never forget her sweet face.

I got up, took a few steps, and stood in front of the mirror where I was able to see the color of the sky in the reflection. I shook my head and felt really happy because I had everything I needed and dreamed of. The sun's rays and the beautiful weather made me feel amazing while the scent of the colorful flowers had already spread through the house, increasing my anticipation of spending the rest of the day having fun with my wife.

I walked to the yard and regarded myself blessed since I believed I had everything a simple man looked for in his life. I remained stable staring at the large cedar trees, gazing toward the whole neighborhood which was covered by the colors and the smells of serenity. I would never forget that unique beauty.

May was my favorite month because everything looked marvelous and the people seemed different. The funny, cheerful mood had managed to survive from the severe winter as I, and countless other people looked forward to joining spring's company.

That season had a unique way to make me behave better while keeping all of my wishes and hopes alive, thinking positively about everything, and hoping for the best. The magic celebration of the environment always affected my life and my thoughts and, as far as I was concerned, every Spring I used to become friendlier and more patient with everyone.

"My crazy father just called," Alyson said.

"Is everything okay?" I was curious.

"He invited us for Frisbee!" Alyson exclaimed. She sounded upset.

I couldn't stop laughing and I couldn't stop wondering again about how lucky I was since even her funny grimace made her look fabulous.

We were in our mid-twenties; we were seeking other things to do and, in addition to that, we both hated Frisbee.

"Let's go," she said.

We always loved having picnics at the national park--we adored feeling lost in central park while glancing at the peaceful lake which was covered by countless white and purple water lilies. Nina and George, our best friends, would join us that day.

"I forgot the wine." Alyson shook her head and bit her lips.

"I'll get it."

The moment I opened the white front door of our house, Alyson stood behind me and started teasing me. While I was searching for the wine in the kitchen, I felt myself losing my balance and immediately looked outside the small window of our small, dark room, catching myself on the small table. I never liked that room since I always felt it was like being in prison, but I could never believe that those four yellow walls and the concrete would save both of us as well.

"What is happening?" my wife asked fearfully.

"I have no idea."

The following seconds I thought I was watching a movie. Alyson came next to me and started screaming and calling for help, holding me tight. Then, she looked up at me and I realized that I had to take over and reassure her that things would be fine, and make her feel safe too.

The moment I rested my jaw on her head, trying to think of a plan to get us out of there, I thought I saw something weird in the sky. I glanced upon the sky again, but a few seconds later, I saw a huge wave of fire wrapping the whole place up while coming closer to us. When it started swallowing everything, I felt absolute fear running in my veins since I believed that death was looking forward to meeting us. Meanwhile, our hopes had already vanished and we both thought we would die.

Impulsively and without losing any further time, we fell on our knees and began screaming, praying to God to save us. The echo of the strong, hot wind along with the horrifying sound of the broken glass and the chilling noise of the destruction of the rest of the things in our house, combined with the sound of the collapsing of our neighborhood's houses made things terrifying.

I had already lost hope while my instincts were struggling to keep both of us alive. I was holding my wife's head in my arms as I was trying to calm her and didn't stop caressing her hair, telling her that everything was good and we would make it.

I could neither open my eyes nor could I make a step and, during the critical moments, I realized that I would never forget the presence of death. The people who were trying to protect themselves while screaming and calling for help would haunt my mind forever.

In a flash, our house caught fire and I rushed to get us out, neglecting the danger of being hurt. But we were lucky because the huge wave of fire was gone and I had the illusion that the nightmare had come to an end.

The following moments we remained still and silent but, after a while, we started walking down the accursed street. We could see dead people, burned human beings lying on the road, assuming they were all trying to get into their houses but, apparently, they didn't have the time they needed to save themselves.

We began calling for help and although we knew that no help would come, we didn't give up.

I held my wife's hand tight and we continued walking around the streets while with every step we took, we felt we were coming closer to the paths of hell.

Suddenly, the black color settled in front of our eyes; the extremely hot wind brought the dust and the ash in front of our faces. The smell of burning flesh was horrible. We couldn't breathe.

The fire carried on destroying everything. Our house was still on fire and so was the rest of our previously wonderful neighborhood. I just couldn't believe it.

"The city, the state, the entire world came across the final destruction because of the sun's explosion. All the scientists had warned us." My wife believed that the sun exploded, but I wasn't sure about that. Wouldn't we be dead?

As minutes passed by, the temperature kept increasing and we could hardly walk. After a while, we felt we couldn't move any longer since our bodies continued losing energy very fast. The sweat didn't stop running down our skins as we both felt like being trapped in a tank of boiled water. We could still tolerate the physical pain, but, normally, after a few minutes of this, we should have been dead.

Even though we were lucky enough to avoid the huge flames of fire, we couldn't escape from the burning hell that had come up.

Alyson fainted and I sat down on the burning road while I placed her head on my legs, thinking of the wonderful moments we had shared. Then, I rolled my eyes and felt the need to pray to God.

The moment I looked up at the sky, I froze. It was like seeing a burning broken glass; I could never imagine I would see something like that. There was no sky anymore since everything up there had turned red and was tearing apart. It looked like an open, burning gate.

Meanwhile, I started wondering about the creatures I had seen a few minutes before the tragedy. They were flying in the sky while having their eyes locked on earth. They looked like human beings and, although I wasn't able to see their faces, I was sure they were plenty of them.

I was scared to death. We had lost everything and, very soon, we would die too. I fixed my eyes on my wife's face and, then, I started writing my last words in this world, with a small white rock on the street, leaving my notes behind to those who would make it.

Yorkshire, U.K.

Nancy ran to Ryan and hid in his arms, her lips quivering in fear. She rested her head on his chest; her blonde hair covering the pain of his soul and the tears of hopelessness.

"What did you see?" Ryan asked.

"I saw the same thing again." Nancy was scared to death.

Although Nancy and Ryan loved summer walks, that year they abstained from strolling in the forest during their free time. They stopped enjoying their lovely moments under the stars of the peaceful, summer nights and they remained in their small, white house –a mile outside of town--gazing at the beautiful, large maple trees.

The last month, the residents of Criston Valley had become curious about the charming couple and since everyone knew their story, they couldn't stop wondering whether everything was fine or not. No one would forget the determination Nancy and Ryan had shown even as teenagers to stay together forever.

In their early twenties, Nancy and Ryan got married and, since then, ten years had already passed. They loved one another and never gave up doing their best to maintain the flames of love in their marriage.

The beautiful couple had managed to steal the attention of the small town since they were young, helpful, and kind with everyone.

***

"What is it, baby?" Nancy was shaking, she was looking up at the sky and the shinning stars.

"What is it, Nancy?" Ryan asked again.

"He told me they are coming," she whispered, shivering.

"Who told you that?" Ryan came closer and stood in front of her.

"The handsome man with the black clothes and the dark face. I think he can read my mind. I can't explain it but, anyway, they are here now. I saw their traces in the sky."

Ryan didn't know how to respond. He pulled his wife close and hugged her.

"They decided to take over. Remember my words-- they can't kill you during the daylight," Nancy said.

"What..." Ryan shook his head while his wife gazed at her husband and stepped back.

Nancy waved at him as a cold smile formed on her sweet face. The moment her eyes released the tears of their separation, Ryan realized he would never see her again. He sensed it was the last time he would talk with his wife, and he always trusted his instincts.

"During the night, they can't hurt you under the ground," Nancy said seriously.

He tried to take his wife in his arms for one last time, but in vain. Nancy pushed him away and looked angrily at his face. Ryan seemed like a soulless, muscular figure, unable to accept the truth.

"We have to see a doctor," Ryan intoned.

Nancy's skin flushed red and the temperature of her body started increasing dramatically.

"What's happening, baby?" Ryan felt helpless. He was panicked, ready to scream for help.

In a flash, huge flames of fire wrapped her body as she looked at him in silence. His presence and love gave Nancy the strength she needed to deal with the pain and the devils of infinity.

"I will always love you," she whispered.

The moment he rushed to save his wife, her body turned into ash, and he began screaming her name and calling for help. Ryan fell on the floor and kept yelling.

In the distance, Ryan could hear the people of the small town calling for help and begging for someone to save their lives. When he stood up, he could hear nothing and no one.

In the following minutes, the sun's rays revealed the tragic reality and the tears in his eyes. Ryan was sure he would remember that terrible morning of June for the rest of his life.

Without knowing what to do, where to go and, mainly, what was happening, he regarded he had no reason to keep on living in a world without hope.

**

Immediately after the first critical moments of the invisible invasion, Ryan drove toward the small, graphic town and during the course he couldn't stop thinking of his wife. He couldn't control his feelings and his thoughts, knowing that he would have to move on with his life, accepting silently Nancy's absence.

When Ryan reached the main square of Criston Valley, he was taken aback. Everything had changed. Everything was extremely quiet.

Ryan stopped the car and carried on gazing at the silent chaos while wondering about the whole situation, worrying about the future.

He got off his car and felt the hot wind on his face which kept spreading ash all over the place. He looked around him and his sight focused on the large windows of the city hall where he could see smoke. There was nothing but an empty city.

"Help me, please."

Ryan turned back and smiled. He walked toward the small bakery shop and a little girl rushed to hide in his arms. The tall, muscular man knelt as the girl hugged him tight. Ryan caressed the back of the frightened girl softly, and the moment he stared at her blue eyes, he already knew what she had gone through.

"What's your name?" Ryan asked.

"Jamie..." the girl whispered.

"How old are you, Jamie?" Ryan wanted to calm her.

"I'm four." The little girl hid in his shirt and started breathing normally.

"Where is your mother?" Ryan wanted to make sure Jamie was there alone.

"I don't know, she said she would be back soon, but she never appeared." Jamie laid her head on his chest and felt safe.

Ryan held her tight and then took the girl in his arms, walking toward his black car. The girl's reaction confirmed his belief about her mother's luck and, from that moment, he never mentioned anything about Jamie's family again.

They got in the car and drove around the city where they could see nothing but closed shops, empty roads and many abandoned cars left in the middle of the streets.

The police station looked like a deserted place; the absolute silence had taken over as the smell of the smoke was still intense and the ash had become one with the sweat which kept running down their faces.

When Ryan realized that he was not going to find someone to help them out, he drove toward the freeway, hoping to meet a person who would be able to give the answers he was seeking for. Ryan looked at Jamie and was determined to live on. His purpose was to keep this girl safe and he would do his best to achieve his goal.

***

Green Valley was the biggest city of the South and Ryan was sure he would get the answers he was looking for. When they reached the police station, Ryan caressed Jamie's black hair and the little girl woke up.

"You were sleeping for almost two hours, young lady," Ryan said as he was trying to pull himself back together.

"Where are we?" Jamie focused her sight on Ryan

and he rested his eyes on hers.

"Green Valley…" Ryan said.

"Where are the people?" Jamie asked.

"They must be sleeping." Ryan didn't know what to say.

The city was lifeless; there was nothing left to remind them the centre of life and civilization. Instead of noise and traffic, there was only quietness. The beautiful buildings, the incredible library, the theatres, the shops and the streets were empty.

Ryan and Jamie got out of the car and walked together, wishing they would run into some other people like them. They could hear nothing other than the small birds on the large maple trees across their sights and that made them freeze. The feeling of being alone in a world without communication became dangerous since it could crash their hearts and souls like crumbling a dry leaf into their hands.

After strolling in the city for hours, Ryan came across despair and countless, silent questions which were ready to haunt his hopes and positive thoughts.

Jamie was searching for her favorite chocolates while Ryan was still gazing at his new friend, thinking of their options. In a flash he rolled his eyes and leaned against the white door of the small, colorful candy shop while his mind traveled back to time, searching for his beloved wife.

"During the night, under the ground they can't touch you," Nancy had told him.

He remembered their last moments and the tears of the pain caused by her cruel death made their appearance on his red cheeks.

Soon, the dark would cover everything and they had to find a shelter.

"Is everything okay, Ryan?" the girl asked.

"Everything is good, Jamie." Ryan swept his tears

away and smiled at his sweet little friend.

***

Five months had passed since Ryan and Jamie lost their families and for more than one hundred days they had been searching for something that would make them hope. Every day they used to drive for many hours to find someone, but every afternoon they used to run into disappointment again.

They didn't have to worry about food, gas and water since they could find everything they wanted. The entire material world belonged to them, but they would both trade everything they had to get their lives and their people back.

As much as Ryan desired to hope that things would change for the better, the whole situation insisted on killing all of his wishes and dreams. The fact that he had to take care of a child and to be optimistic for her sake as well drove him mad; he suffocated, and there was nothing he could do.

"I'm cold," Jamie whispered.

Ryan grabbed the brown blanket from the broken closet and covered Jamie's cold body. They were hiding in a small cavity, next to the basement under the church of their home town, looking forward to meeting the daylight. The humidity and the disgusting smell kept assaulting their noses, but they had nowhere else to go. After their research, they rushed to get down the stairs to hide from the dark. Before reaching their shelter, the helpless man sensed the presence of those who destroyed everything. His heart started beating faster and he couldn't stop shaking. He felt someone was watching them, waiting for their next move so as to trap them and finally kill them, and putting an end to their pathetic lives.

When the girl fell asleep, Ryan went up there again and prayed to God to save Jamie. He took a few steps toward the window and waited in silence. Soon, Ryan was able to hear the speakers, but he couldn't understand what they were saying. His curiosity made him come closer to the truth and he dared to face those who were responsible for the destruction of humanity.

The moment he looked outside, he could see nothing but their traces. It was like seeing tiny, black vortexes in the air. Ryan shook his head. He couldn't find the appropriate words to describe what he was looking at. He was scared to death, but he had to be strong for Jamie.

***

The unexpected change of the climate and the severe winter had managed to haunt their lives since the bad weather conditions and the snow had restricted them to staying in a dim basement. The last three days they hadn't moved at all because of the snow that had covered everything, and because of the dense fog which insisted hiding the daylight, bringing the dark and the despair earlier than ever into their lives.

"It's freaking freezing and I'm cold, Ryan," the sweet girl murmured.

Jamie was shaking, her skin had turned red and Ryan realized that she needed help; he was in desperate need of painkillers and drugs since a fever was killing her. Jamie was very sick and Ryan was sure they were not going to make it. When he touched Jamie's forehead, Ryan knew what he had to do.

"I will fix it, baby," he said.

Ryan took Jamie in his arms and stepped in the basement of the church. He walked slowly toward the stairs while Jamie had already fallen asleep on his chest. It was the time to meet the beings with the black clothes, those who had stolen his wife's life.

Ryan opened the large door of the church and walked outside. The following minutes, he remained still, gazing at the confusing scene. It was a very beautiful picture since the bare maple trees, the fields, the cars they used to drive and the deserted houses were covered by the snow.

When Ryan looked up at the sky, he believed that the snowflakes were showing him the path to heaven. He smiled and then he stared at Jamie who was still sleeping. Ryan kissed her forehead, remembering Nancy's words about life and God. "No one can make us part. I will be waiting for you somewhere up there." They were sitting comfortably in the wooden chairs in their yard; it was the last night they shared.

"Look at the maple trees; they have something weird on them. Their leaves are strange." She had told him to make him forget her words, enjoying their last moments.

Then, again, Ryan remembered her words.

"During the night, under the ground, they can't hurt you."

Ryan couldn't fight anymore--everything was against their survival. He was looking forward to seeing his wife again.

"I will never forget you, Jamie," he whispered.

The moment he kissed Jamie's forehead for the last time, Ryan felt weird. He tried to look around him but it was unfeasible. He closed his eyes and thought he was losing his mind and the contact with reality. He wanted to scream since he felt losing his memories and all the moments he had spent on earth. It was like losing his identity, like he had never been a human being.

What's happening? Ryan wondered.

The human-like beings with the black clothes appeared in front of him and smiled at him. They were too many, maybe fifty of them. They were all men, taller than the humans and very beautiful. Ryan's sight focused on the little girl and felt Jamie's body warm as never before.

"I am coming, Nancy. I am coming with our new friend," Ryan said.

Huge flames of fire wrapped their bodies while

Ryan gazed at Jamie. The fever had already killed her--
there was no pain. Their souls left their bodies. Ryan and
Jamie were finally released while the dark secret was
buried under the ash of the temples of their precious hearts.
There was nothing else left. The black angels had done
their work, and their traces were everywhere.

Sydney, Australia

er beautiful, long fingers slept on the yellow curtains as her blue eyes kept searching for the prince she was waiting for. Her mind continued making plans for the future whereas the sun's rays ran into her pale face, enlightening her complexion and changing her mood.

The girl loved looking outside; she liked watching the beautiful valley across their lovely farm. She felt like being a part of a wonderful picture where the green color along with the rest of the colors of the spring had started dominating in the whole area. She pulled her blonde hair back while her long, yellow dress made her look like Dimitra, the ancient Greek goddess of agriculture and fertility.

The young girl turned back and smiled at her mother who liked staring at her daughter in silence, trying to guess her thoughts. Although her daughter had never revealed her inner feelings, she could understand and explain the signs of love.

"It's nice being in love, but we have many things to do," the mother said vaguely.

The middle-aged woman took off her white coat and left it on the chair while she came closer to her daughter and caressed her sweet face.

"There is not only Patrick in your life, Abby," she said.

"I know that, Mother," Abby answered angrily.

"Since dinner is ready, I want you to call your father." The woman abstained from saying anything else because she hated seeing her daughter defensive, being unwilling to talk about her relationship.

"Yes, Mother," Abby whispered.

"That's great, thank you, baby." The woman knew that she had to wait for her daughter's acceptance.

"I'm going right now."

"Okay, honey."

Her mother gave her daughter her coat and held her right hand, looking into her eyes, trying to make the introduction for those she was planning to say, but found very difficult to mention since the girl always avoided discussing with her mother about boys.

"Abby, you are only sixteen. I know that you like Patrick and I think he is a good kid, but I don't want you to rush doing something that you might regret or don't want," she said seriously.

"Mom, take it easy, I'm still a virgin." Abby sounded nervous.

"I just want to tell you that it's your decision. Don't let anyone decide for you." Her mother smiled and hugged her daughter, feeling relieved.

"I know what I'm doing, Mom. You will have to trust me." Abby said.

"I trust you, baby." She caressed her hair and laughed. She hesitated to ask directly her daughter about her relationship with the teenage boy, but she couldn't postpone their conversation either.

"I'm going to call Dad," Abby said.

"That would be great, honey."

The young girl put on the white coat and closed the white door behind her, walking slowly toward the stairs of the spacious yard. The sun hid behind the white clouds and the cool air reminded Abby of the cold days of the winter. But the beautiful valley had already put on the dress with the intense colors of light, joy and optimism. One sight upon the large trees was enough to come across euphoria. Her blue eyes had turned into a round mirror, reflecting the magic power of the nature.

Abby took a few steps and stared at the small goose while she didn't miss to wave and smile at her favorite friend. When she heard the sound of the tractor upon the hill, she ran toward her father, feeling free and happy. Her long hair was flying in the air as she loved running among the tall, dry canes. Abby could smell the scent of the rain in the air and hated the thought of walking in the mud again. She loved the heat and looked forward to seeing the hot, sunny days.

Out of the blue, Abby felt weird. She stopped and looked up at the sky, wondering about the large shadow which flew above her and hid the daylight from her sight. She felt there was something going on; she had goosebumps and she couldn't hear the sound of her father's tractor anymore. The moment she saw all the black birds in the sky forming a huge, dark cloud, Abby started laughing nervously.

The beautiful girl grabbed a small piece of a dry cane and ripped it up in her cold hands in an effort to expel the fear which tried to invade her peaceful world. Abby started walking again and was soon able to see the black birds resting on the red track. The absence of her father made her worry and she didn't waste her time. She began calling him by her pet name for him.

"Super Dad!" Abby sounded scared.

The girl ran over the field, making circles around their large farm. The moment she realized she had searched everywhere, she went back at her father's track where she took a deep breath and sat down on the ground, hoping that soon she would find her father. The birds were eating the seeds of the corn from the jagged ground, but she didn't have the courage to stand up and make them leave.

"Super Dad!" the girl screamed again.

Abby got up and started looking for her father again until she heard her mother screaming for help.

"Mom?" Abby was taken aback. She started shaking, unable to see her mother from where she was.

"Abby, run baby, they will kill you!" her mother shouted.

Abby panicked and started running toward the big house to help her mother. Although the distance she had to go was not more than two hundred meters, it seemed to be far away and, every minute that passed by, Abby felt she was coming closer to death. The moment she heard her mother begging for mercy she froze in fear, everything became dark and the only thing she wanted was to save her mom.

Suddenly, she fell on a tall man who stood unwavering in the middle of the farm, hidden by the canes, and she crashed onto the rough ground.

"Super Dad?" Abby asked, trying to stand up.

"What is happening, Dad?" Abby asked again while the tall, beautiful man Abby thought was her father said nothing.

"Where is Mom, Dad?" As she rose, Abby glanced at the canes and saw a man lying on the ground. His blue shirt and his bright blue jeans were covered by his blood and all she wanted was to scream. His brown hat kept covering his hair, but she could see his eyes. She would never forget the dead blue color of her father's eyes.

"She was useless," the tall man said.

"What did you say?" Abby was looking at a muscular man with a lifeless facial expression and yellow eyes.

"I am Leonim and your father was useless too." His voice made her chill as her face turned red and her legs started shaking.

"Who are you?" Abby asked, dread in her voice.

"I told you, I am Leonim." He stretched out his arm and offered his hand while Abby started to run up the hill toward the red tractor.

Leonim reappeared before her, stopping her in her tracks.

"How did you do that?" she whispered.

"You are so beautiful," Leonim said.

Abby started screaming for help but in vain.

"What are you? What do you want?" She had no time to think of anything other than saving her life.

The tall man placed his hands on her face and she froze. Abby was living a hell and she could do nothing to make this stop.

"You will become the mother of my children." Leonim said.

Abby pushed him back as hard as she could and tried to get away. She wanted to hurt him, but she was not able to harm him.

"I will kill you!" Abby shouted. He laid a gentle hand on her head, and she lost consciousness. She would never remember anything again.

***

When Abby woke up, she got up from the bed and started walking around the spacious bedroom. She was naked and lovely. She loved touching her belly, making dreams and plans for the future.

"How are you, my lord?" Abby was different.

"Everything is good." Leonim sounded happy.

"That's wonderful." She sounded proud of him.

"How is my son?" Leonim asked.

"He is getting bigger," Abby said, caressing her belly.

Leonim was impatient to make his own world with his own offspring. He knew that Marc would be prepared to face him. Leonim's children, compared to the new Alphas, had to be stronger to kill them. He felt he had to hurry. Although he had been given a second chance, he had given up on the trust he was offered long ago.

Trapped in Timelessness
Shadows of the Past

Sara pulled her black, wet hair away from her beautiful face and wrapped her well-shaped body with a blue towel. When she got out of the bathroom, everything seemed the same as she walked around her cramped house in silence. The anxious woman took a few steps toward the living room and searched the silent home, wondering about their decision to move into a quiet village which looked like a spooky place. Soon she discovered there was nothing strange taking place in her precious shelter.

The strong wind made the large sycamores lean toward the orange tile roof and the chilly noise caused her a weird feeling as she started shaking, losing the net of safety she was striving to retain. She looked outside the kitchen window and saw that the sun was hiding behind the large mountains opposite the house. The dark had already begun covering everything she could see, and of course the naked, dry valley in front of her eyes. The fog around the lake near the house and the freezing night looked willing to accommodate the shadows of the past and destroy her peaceful life.

Sara tried to catch her breath and get past her fears as she placed her fingers on her head, looking ready to scream. She stretched out her arms to pull the curtains shut to avoid seeing outside the frightening valley when her sight locked on the cold glass of the window. *I am sorry,* she read and, immediately, her fingers left the soft, brown curtains from her hands and she stepped back in shock.

Impulsively, she turned on all the lights and the TV and grabbed her cell phone from the small table. The cold, white tile floor had trapped her wet footsteps on it, but she was sure she had cleaned everything and the long, white

111

hairs there were definitely not hers. She knelt and gazed at them, feeling the cold atmosphere ready to haunt her soul. Her body sensed the presence of something evil, and her skin turned white like the lonely clouds of optimism in the sky during the cold days of the winter. Sara looked at the window again.

"Oh my God..." she whispered as her left hand sealed her mouth.

"I'm sorry."-A skinny, naked boy stood outside the glass, looking at her. The kid was maybe four or five years old and looked like a bleeding angel.

"What, who are you?"

The unexpected guest disappeared. Sara remained on the floor, tears running down her face.

"Sara, Sara what happened?"

Rick came in the house and rushed to Sara. He knelt next to his wife and held her head in his arms, making her feel secure and loved.

"Did you see it again?" Rick asked.

Sara nodded, trying to forget what she saw earlier and for the last two days. Her husband caressed her hair and tried to calm her. He felt desperate, unable to help her overcome the dangerous games of her mind.

Rick recalled the moment they stepped into their house--two months ago--when everything seemed wonderful. They had decided to make a new beginning in the countryside since they both regarded that the exhausting, demanding life in New York City had stolen their energy, time and love. At the time they started finding their rhythms and discovering the joy of living carefree moments again, the shadows of the past came back to haunt them.

"I don't want to live in this house anymore, Rick," Sara said.

"That's okay, baby, let me take care of everything," Rick reassured her.

They stood up, still embracing. The young couple got rid of the initial shock and the entire experience but, unfortunately, nothing was over because everything had just started; the nightmare was ready to settle in their house.

"Put your clothes on while I make us some coffee," Rick said.

"Okay, baby."

Sara left his hand and swept her face heading toward the stairs where she came across the boy she saw earlier in the living room.

"Sara…" Rick's voice, but faint.

The frightened woman ran into the kitchen. Her husband was lying on the floor, trying to stop the blood flowing from his belly with a towel he'd somehow grabbed before he fell.

"Rick!" She knelt beside him and helped.

"You will be fine, everything is good." Sara said.

Her husband sat up, having stemmed the bleeding.

"Who said that?" An old woman said.

When Sara heard the chilling voice, she froze inside, and looked toward the sound.

They stared at an old, ugly woman who looked steadily at them. Rick pushed himself to stand up and fight against the shadows of hell. Although the nasty cut had stolen his strength, he was not eager to surrender.

"Who are you?" Sara asked, trembling. Her courage had gone.

The gaunt woman looked capable of anything, and was waiting for their reaction. She wore a faded black dress and her black eyes were hooked on the young couple. Her long, white hair kept hiding the countless wrinkles on her skin, covering her ugly face, trying to bury the signs of death, pain and evil.

"I never wanted that girl," the old woman snapped.

"What did she do?" Rick asked angrily, trying very

hard to stay on his feet.

Sara had gotten up and was throwing whatever came to hand at on the intruder in a vain effort to drive her away. In the meantime, Rick was trying to reach the table.

"She gave birth to this baby. She shouldn't have done that," the old woman said.

The skinny boy appeared next to his grandmother, making the old woman mad. The boy held the aged woman's left hand and smiled at Sara and Rick.

"What do you want from us? Leave us alone!" Sara said angrily.

"That boy is the devil and I want to get rid of him," the old woman said. She looked at Rick's wound and smiled.

In a flash, Sara grabbed the knife from the bench and tried to kill the invader.

"Go to hell!"

The knife passed right through, leaving her unharmed. The cursed shadow of the past slapped Sara and the young woman fell on the floor, wondering about the old woman's strength. Rick lost his balance and fell next to her. The pain was horrible and the bleeding had started again. "You are not going anywhere."

The deadly woman took the knife and reached Sara. Suddenly, the skinny boy held his grandmother's hand and they both vanished, leaving the young couple the chance to fight against time and fate.

There was no one in the house except Sara and Rick. She grabbed the phone and called for help.

***

Sara closed the white door behind her and took off her brown coat. She turned off the lights and walked to the window of the kitchen. The sun's rays had invaded the house, making her sight focus on the red floor. The moment she stared at the blood, she remembered Rick and everything that took place in their house the previous night, and then all those incredible moments she had shared in the past along with her husband.

With no further delay, Sara swept her tears away and moved toward the bedroom to get some of her and Rick's things. She threw them into a black bag and rushed to get out of there since every minute that passed by, she felt she was coming closer to hell.

The moment she got down the stairs and stood in front of the living room, she froze in fear, and started shaking. Sara knelt and read the strange words written with her husband's blood, wondering whether the weird sign was there earlier or not. *Under the poplar tree.*

The young woman got up, grabbed her coat and bag and ran toward the front door. She turned back and looked around her, thinking of the nightmare she had lived in that house. "We are not coming back," she whispered and rushed to get out there.

The following day workers started digging out the ground to reveal the truth and satisfy Sara's curiosity. Before long, the poplar tree was down and Sara was looking forward to coming closer to the secrets of the past. She couldn't stop wondering about the weird sign; she couldn't get it out of her mind.

"Who told you?"

Sara looked back and saw a young blonde woman next to her, smiling kindly at her.

"I beg your pardon?" Sara asked.

"Who told you?" The unknown woman asked again.

Sara kept looking at the stranger, thinking of her words.

"Is he dead?" the unknown woman asked again.

The blonde woman lit a cigarette and gazed at the workers.

Sara became nervous.

"Your husband, is he dead?" the stranger asked.

"Who are you?" Sara was taken aback.

"I am looking for my boy. Thank you for everything," she said.

The man with the bright blue pants waved at Sara and she went over to join him. The digging had stopped.

"I think we should call the police," the worker said.

"Why, what happened?" Sara asked.

"We found a human body."

***

After many hours, the police officers found out everything. A boy had been buried alive by his own grandmother while the mother of the child had disappeared and was still missing. Some of the aged residents claimed that there were some rumors concerning the daughter of the murderer. They mentioned that the woman was raped and gave birth to a child and no one had seen her since. Some of them regarded that she was locked in the basement for years, but none of the villagers dared to talk to her mother or the police. Nothing else was ever known and, although the event had taken place forty years ago, the photo of the mother was still in a file in the black closet of the police station among with the rest of the missing person's cases. Mrs. Saradin, the daughter's teacher in school had mentioned her absence, but no one dealt with her case seriously.

When Sara looked at the photo of the missing woman, she froze in fear. She was sure that this was the woman she was talking with the day that the workers started bringing the light to the dark secret hidden on their land.

***

Sara held tight to Rick's hand and embraced him. Her husband kissed her forehead and looked into her lustrous eyes.

"I love you," Rick said.

"I love you too." Sara half-closed her eyes and kissed him.

116

They made love in the house Sara had said she would never be back to while the dark had already blanketed the whole area.

A few hours later, Sara got up from the bed and put her clothes on while Rick followed her toward the kitchen. When the young woman looked at the place where the body of the boy had been found, Sara saw the old woman gazing at her angrily, and then she started coming toward their house.

"Rick!" Sara was scared to death.

"What happened?" Rick was surprised.

They got out of the house while the shadow of the past carried on following them. They couldn't run since Rick was injured and shouldn't press his body. They reached the lake and got into the water to escape, stopping to rest at a large rock. In a few hours, the daylight would reveal everything. They would find out they were stranded in the shelter where Leona and Nick were trapped for many years.

The following day they realized that everything had changed and they were not alone anymore. They belonged to a team and were safe.

End

About the Author:

A.A Schenna was born on May 8, 1982 and currently lives with his partner Maria in Athens, Greece. As a child, A.A dreamed of being a cardiac surgeon. Later, Schenna realized that this was not what he wanted.

Writing has always been his greatest pleasure. When he doesn't write action, adventure, romance stories or anything else, he reads everything.
Schenna admires all the writers he comes across and enjoys talking about books and magazines.

A.A loves meeting new people and discovering new places.

Acknowledgements:

I would like to thank author and Editor in Chief KC Sprayberry for trusting me while supporting my writing career. Thank you, Kathi; I will never forget your help. Many thanks to Cynthia Ley and Solstice Publishing.

Social Media Links:

Website: www.aaschenna.com

Facebook: https://www.facebook.com/pages/AA-Schenna/701740166542505?ref=hl

Twitter: https://twitter.com/ASchenna